Spire Wilderness

A Dragon Spawn Novella
(Commander Hapker's Origin Story)

By Dawn Ross
© 2024

"Some journeys take us far from home.
Some adventures lead us to our destiny."
— **CS Lewis**

Spire Wilderness

A Dragon Spawn Novella
(Commander Hapker's Origin Story)

by Dawn Ross

Cover
The cover art was created by Mijoro Teddy Razafindrazaha. The starry background is a public domain image from NASA. All the images were combined to create the cover by germancreative on fiverr.com, including the paid-for art of the spaceship in the sky.

Special Thanks

I'd like to extend a special thanks to all the beta readers and editors who helped me make this novel shine. And additional thanks to my final editor, Grace Bridges, who has been instrumental in helping me with content and line edits as well as with pointing out opportunities for story improvement.

Spire Wilderness

A Dragon Spawn Novella
by Dawn Ross

1
Dregs of the Universe

The first evening stars glinted above, promising adventure. A sea of spaceships spread out in a jumbled maze below on the Medberian Plain. The setting sun reflected orange light off the metal hulls, making the otherwise flat and barren land glow like a rocky riverbed at twilight. Brighter lights twinkled from a handful of buildings clustered off to the left. The silhouette of the traffic control tower stood among them like a sentinel—grand and majestic.

Perched on a cliff above the edge of the plain, J.D. Hapker marveled at the activity below. A few blinding white flares lit up a vast section of the shipyard as vertical landers dropped in or lifted off. A spaceship approached horizontally, appearing to grow as it neared the runway. Unlike most cargo ships, it had wings, reminding him of a stingray.

He wondered what new and exotic wares this vessel carried. Soft Yaverian cloth? Renganese spices? Household bots from Kesovia? Maybe they transported one of those colossal blackbeasts he'd recently learned about. He couldn't wait to go down there and find out.

He'd visited this remarkable place nearly every day since the start of his Maytime break. Never mind that his parents had forbidden it. *"I don't want you in contact with the dregs of the universe,"* his dad had said. But it only incited his curiosity.

As far as his parents knew, he was camping in the Spire Wilderness with a group of his friends. The wilderness was nice, but this was different—exotic. The collage of mismatched spaceships took his breath away. Even more astounding were those who crewed them. Peculiar people from all over the galaxy came here, hoping to trade their off-world merchandise before moving on to another star system.

One day, he'd journey with them, beyond this ordinary planet.

Dawn Ross

Not for the first time, he imagined what it would be like to join the Prontaean Cooperative. As a spacefaring organization run by hundreds of member worlds, they provided intergalactic services such as ship rescue, policing, and scientific ventures. Too bad he couldn't learn more from a Cooperative officer here since their ships only landed at a larger and fancier spaceport farther away.

He immersed himself in daydreaming as Pholatia's two moons chased each other across the sky. They were small, mere smudges of light although in their full phase. Most of the stars were equally pale from nearby light pollution. Only the uppermost star in the Adona constellation sparkled brightly. The second most visible was actually two stars close together. And the one beside it was a distant galaxy.

"Bah!" a voice behind him cried out.

J.D. yelped and jerked away. Fadwa emerged from the shadows. She looked like a ferocious kitten with her teeth bared and her hands curled like claws.

He burst into laughter. "I almost had a heart attack!" he said, playfully smacking her hands away.

"Your eyes!" She covered her mouth and giggled. "They popped out almost."

He laughed. She'd gotten him good this time. But that was alright. He'd get even with her later. Maybe put a blue-tailed skink down the back of her kurta. Those little creatures thrived here on the plain, ships or no. He briefly wondered how many of them had stowed away on the cargo vessels and traveled to new worlds.

"You come, or what?" she asked, her brown eyes gleaming.

He grinned. She returned it by mocking his crooked smile. His cheeks burned as he tried to wipe away the natural lopsidedness of his lips. For whatever reason, his mouth hung low like a frown on one side—or tilted up like a smile on the other, depending on one's perspective—and was more pronounced when he smiled.

Fadwa smacked his arm. "Don't have embarrassment. I like your smile. It's cute."

The heat on his face intensified, but for a different reason. He smiled again, more shyly.

A blurred shape swept in and landed on Fadwa's shoulder. He blinked, knowing what it was but still in awe. In the flash of a

2

shimmering wave, the haze coalesced into a big black bird. Fadwa slid her finger down the side of the animal's head and cooed.

Zahir was her pet, a bird augmented with cybernetics. She'd told him how she'd rescued it from an animal trader on Troitsk, along with other exotic creatures kept in tiny cages. Rather than escape like the others she'd freed, this raven-like bird stuck with her.

"J.D. friend," the bird said through its cybernetic speaker as it tilted his head from side to side.

"That's right," Fadwa replied in a sing-song voice. "J.D. friend." The bird leaned toward him and clicked its beak. "Nice boy" J.D. caressed the side of its neck. "Nice bird."

"Nice bird go now." Zahir activated its camouflage, turning its feathers into a mix of colors that matched the darkened land and sky. Then it flew off.

"Make no trouble!" Fadwa grasped J.D.'s hand and led him down the rocky slope, her ponytail swishing back and forth. He almost pulled away to wipe off his sweaty palms, but he didn't want to hurt her feelings. Besides, he liked holding her hand.

Fadwa had said she was probably eleven years old, or twelve like him. She wasn't sure since she'd lived in space her entire life and didn't know how to convert the Universal Standard to Pholatian dates. J.D. could've done it for her, but she hadn't seemed interested in it enough for him to take the time to do the math.

From the moment he'd met her in the city, he knew she wasn't Pholatian. It wasn't just her flowered dress-like shirt she called a kurta or emerald-colored leggings. Her eyes and hair were too dark and her face too round. And she was thinner than a pond reed. But she resembled his people in every other way—unlike some of the other travelers he'd seen recently. And she was pretty.

She bounded over the rubble like a gazelle compared to his long-legged goofiness. His heart flip-flopped, either out of concern that he'd step between rocks and break his ankle or because she'd invited him to her ship. Probably both.

Hopping from the last boulder, they landed on flat ground. Still hand-in-hand, they raced across the pebbled plain, the crunching under their feet creating an exciting rhythm.

Light from the interior of the nearest ship illuminated their way. He craned his neck to see inside the open cargo hatch. *Just crates.* Nothing interesting.

The ship itself was rather ordinary—oblong like most cargo vessels. Its hatch opened from the side with two propulsion units that jutted from the aft-dorsal. All standard.

Five people sat outside. Other than darker skin tones and tightly curled hair, they also resembled Pholatians. No weird features—at least not that he could see. However, a strange cylindrical contraption stood in the middle of their circle. Its eerie blue glow created a mystical lighting, and it emitted a low plasmic crackle that tickled J.D.'s ears.

"What's that?" He pointed with a tilt of his head.

"What? The thing blue?" she asked using her foreign syntax. "It's an eco-unit, multipurpose."

"What's it do?"

She looked at him like he was daft. "You have no comprehension of eco-units?"

J.D. shrugged. "It depends on what it does."

She cocked her head. "I forget planet-life differences. This gives power, heat, light, and other uses."

Considering the coolness of the evening and how they sat around it, that last one made sense. "Like a campfire?"

"What's campfire?"

J.D. barked a laugh. He wasn't the only one learning new things. "It also emits light and heat, but in a primitive way—with wood and fire."

"Oh." She shrugged. "Thought so."

He side-eyed her, wondering whether she'd really guessed that or if she merely pretended because he'd embarrassed her by laughing. He hadn't meant to make fun. *Maybe I should apologize.*

An upward curve of her lips indicated she wasn't upset. "Come on, slowpoke. We'll never come to my ship if your eyes stick on things."

"They're not stuck," he replied, though he wasn't sure if that was true.

Along the way, they passed a squat man with a long mustache who pulled a wheeled cart. Further on was a group of men with three nostrils and sharply ridged brows. Ambling behind them was an android pieced together with old junk.

The wide spaces between the ships thickened with more than just people. He edged around a motorized chair carrying a woman

4

thinner than Fadwa. Mechanic bots rolled along. Loaders rumbled by. Vehicular transports swerved through.

J.D. swiveled his head, taking it all in. New sights weren't the only things he looked for. Pholatian Protectors patrolled this area. Although the chances of them recognizing him were slim, he didn't want to get caught. Dad would ground him, and J.D. had that class trip to the Chenier Islands coming up.

Almost as exotic as this place, the islands were home to several unique Pholatian animals. For whatever reason, the Komodo from ancient Earth had evolved into something grander here on Pholatia, boasting a larger size, iridescent green and purple skin, thinner physique, and sharper teeth. More than anything, he wanted to meet a dragon in real life.

Fadwa yanked his arm, making him stumble sideways and preventing him from running into a hunched man wearing a dusty brown robe. "Watch out, silly," she said, her eyes sparking with mirth. "They aren't aliens."

"Might as well be," he mumbled.

She giggled.

Despite his silent promise to pay attention to where he was going, he couldn't help but gape at one of the strangest ships he'd seen yet. Most cargo vessels had a distinctive rectangular shape, but this was more rounded. Even odder were its propulsion units. There were four of them, one for each curved corner, and they faced downward, resembling upside-down cups.

Fadwa nudged him—hard. He whipped his head around to her wide eyes. She pointed emphatically to her right. J.D. glanced over to see a pair of Pholatian Protectors headed this direction.

Oh crap. Sergeant Vargo's blond beard and fat nose was unmistakable. The bulky man didn't seem to look this way, but he was as observant as a wolf on the hunt. If he saw J.D., he'd report it.

That would be the end of any more adventures.

J.D. held his breath and hung his head, hoping he hadn't been seen. Fadwa grasped his hand and led him in the opposite direction. Her casual pace grated on the edge of his panic, but he didn't urge her to move faster. No doubt a swift movement would capture the attention of the prowling wolf.

"Are they following?" he asked Fadwa, not daring to turn around.

She peeked over her shoulder a few times, her silence revving up his heart. "Doesn't seem so," she finally said.

J.D. puffed. They navigated through a throng of intriguing people and diverse spaceships. He nearly bumped into a man who looked like a giant ball with legs. Mumbling an apology, he skirted around to catch up with Fadwa.

After passing a half-dozen more vessels, she brought him to an old ship and smiled. She patted its stained and pockmarked hull. "This is *Razeka*."

J.D. grinned. It was just as interesting as he'd hoped. It wasn't as wide as others he'd seen. The cargo hatch was in the rear rather than the side, but it made sense considering its smaller design. Older hull panels with layers upon layers of scorch marks clashed with somewhat newer ones. Some pieces appeared a bit warped. Few bolts matched. He almost called this vessel a flying bucket, but seeing how much her eyes lit up as she showed it to him kept his stupid words locked behind his lips.

"Fadwa," a woman with kind eyes said in a sweet voice. "This is your friend?" She had dark hair like Fadwa's, but wavy. Her willowy figure resembled Fadwa's as well. Her maroon kurta was tattered in places, but serviceable.

"This is J.D.," Fadwa said, and J.D. put on his best smile. "J.D., this is Saba. My mother, but not my mother."

Saba chuckled as she put her arm around Fadwa's shoulder. "We make our own family," she added. "Pleased to meet you, J.D. You both come in, drink tea. Have biscuits too."

J.D. hesitated. They appeared to live on the edge. He didn't want to take away from them but neither did he want to be disrespectful by refusing. He made a mental note to bring them some of his mom's granola cookies the next time he came.

"Come, come," Fadwa said, beckoning him to the hatch. "Come view what my father purchased."

The intensity of her gleeful grin ignited his curiosity. He smiled back, but halted when she froze. Something about the curl of her brows made his hair stand on end. He followed her frozen gaze to a team of Pholatian Protectors headed this direction with purposeful strides.

His chest hitched. Sergeant Vargo must've seen him and sent these men to retrieve him. Either that, his dad figured out he hadn't gone camping and had Protectors out looking for him all along.

He sidestepped away from the ship, not wanting to implicate Fadwa and her family in his wrongdoing, and gulped. *Crap. I'm in huge trouble.*

2
Apprehended

Fadwa almost laughed at the lopsided grin of the boy beside her. She'd never met anyone who was so interested in how she lived. Most people looked at her like she was a space rat. They sometimes even called her as much, especially after seeing her home. But he had gawked at it in the same way as he had the other ships here.

Saba winked at her when J.D. wasn't looking and leaned toward her ear. "You speak true. He's cute," she whispered.

Fadwa's face flushed. She glanced away and bit her lip, hoping J.D. didn't have hearing half as sensitive as hers.

With his gaze still upward as he studied her home, she led him to the cargo hatch. Fadwa used the moment to admire his ear-length hair. She'd seen people with hair the color of sand dunes before, but never with such soft rolling ripples. Such shiny grease-free hair must be one perk of living on a planet with so much water.

She turned away so he wouldn't catch her staring at him like a loony, then glimpsed something that made her throat hitch. Four white-uniformed Pholatian Protectors stormed toward her ship with her father restrained between them. Parvaz, Aymen, and Taz were there too. Aymen's eyes blazed like torches while Parvaz hung his head. Taz's brows curled as though confused while her father looked straight ahead with a stubborn tilt to his chin.

J.D. stepped away. *He's leaving?* The hurt in her heart flared to choler. She shot him a dirty look. *Craven.*

He wagged his head and pointed at himself. His crooked lips moved, but she didn't know the Universal Language well enough to read them. If he had made any sound—even a whisper—she would've heard him even if he were four times farther away. It hardly mattered now. She had no interest in hearing excuses for his spineless behavior.

8

He surprised her by putting himself before the soldiers. They kept coming, not bothering to look at him. He stumbled aside, confusion curling his brow.

Oh! He thought they were here for him. What a dummy. Didn't he know they had her father? *Don't be a ninny.* He couldn't have known since he hadn't met him yet.

Saba stepped protectively in front of Fadwa as the men approached. "What is this about?" The strain in her voice gave away her distress.

The tallest and broadest of the protectors stomped forward. He looked Saba up and down with a depreciative glint that made Fadwa's insides knot with outrage. "Mister Rafayet here was caught purchasing illegal goods." His wide mouth curled in distaste.

"I have no knowledge of lawbreaks." Her dad's golden eyes flared like the glowing moons of Plixier, yet he didn't struggle against them. The long, straight black hair on his head and chin remained as fixed as his demeanor. It was just like him to present a collected confidence, with only his eyes giving away his mood. She couldn't fathom how he managed it when her temper seethed like a plasma vortex.

The lead protector shot a glower over his shoulder. "Ignorance is no excuse for breaking the law. Unless you came here illegally as well, you should have a copy of our country's ordinances."

"You can't expect we recall the whole hundred thousand words."

"Tell him, Father!" Fadwa shouted.

The lead protector ignored her and sneered at her father. "If you weren't able to comply, you shouldn't have come."

Fadwa hissed. Saba folded her arms. Her attempt to appear defiant looked more like uncertainty. "What did you purchase?"

"Foodstuff," her father snapped.

"Food?" Fadwa's ire spiked. "You arrest him over food?" She lurched forward, ready to lash out at this man.

Saba held her back. "Calm yourself," she whispered in Fadwa's ear. "Anger won't help."

Fadwa reluctantly stilled. Saba straightened. "Since when is it illegal?" she asked the lead protector.

"Certain goods are not permitted to leave this planet," the man replied. He marched toward Saba like a combat bot, hard and purposeful. "Now, move aside while we search your ship."

"You can't do—" Saba cut off as the protector shouldered her.

"We most certainly can."

He barged through the open hatch. When two other protectors followed him, Fadwa realized more protectors had come. There were eight now. Four with her father and friends and four marching onto her ship.

She scowled back and forth between her father and Saba, wondering why they didn't protest. *This can't be happening!* They'd been treated with prejudice before, but never arrested. Unlike many other cargo captains she knew, her father always did his best to obey the rules, even when those rules were ridiculously complex.

"Wait!" a young voice called out. "You must have a warrant."

Fadwa's mouth dropped open as J.D. darted in after the protectors with fists clenched. A protector just as tall as the leader but not as bulky grasped him and steered him out. When he let go, J.D. attempted to rush right back in. The man flung out his arm, making J.D. stumble and fall on his butt.

"Stay out of this, kid!" the man said. "Or you'll get hurt."

J.D. bounded to his feet. "My dad is Legislator Hapker!"

The man narrowed his eyes. The lead protector reappeared with hands on hips. "Legislator Hapker's kid, huh? I bet he'll want to know why you're with these rogues."

"They're my friends."

The leader tsked. "Your father will be even less pleased to learn that. But I'll tell you what. Leave now, and I won't tell him."

"I'm not leaving to let you break the law."

Fadwa eyed J.D. with new admiration. She didn't know what a legislator was, but it sounded important. Having one on her family's side might help get her father out of this.

"For your information, kid, the law applies differently to these outsiders. Docking protocols allow us to investigate any potential criminal activity without a warrant. After all, we can't wait around and give these rogues a chance to leave before facing the consequences."

Fadwa's heart sank. J.D.'s shoulders slumped and his lopsided mouth turned down.

Another protector stepped out from the ship. "We found it, Sir."
Found it? Fadwa frowned.

"That doesn't surprise me, Private." The lead protector shot them all an *I've-got-you-now* look.

"Ah, perfect. Having one of our nano-food fabricors is enough to lock all of you away for at least a year."

"Wait!" her father said, finally losing his cool and echoing the outrage burning in her chest. "We have a permit for purchase. We filed paperwork and declared it for customs."

"I doubt that, but we'll check anyway. For now, you're all under arrest. Including you ma'am."

Saba stepped back. "Me? I did nothing."

"We're detaining you until we receive confirmation of your *legal* purchase."

"But my daughter," Fadwa's father said. "Surely you won't lock up a child or leave her here solus."

The lead protector eyed her, making her feel like kibble. Her ire flared.

"We'll take her to a juvenile detention center," the soldier replied. Even though he didn't smile, she could see it in his eyes.

J.D.'s expression exploded into horror. "You can't! I saw the news. I know how horrible that place is."

The soldier rolled his eyes. "That was an isolated incident sensationalized by the media."

Fadwa didn't believe him. The horror stamped on J.D.'s face indicated he didn't either. "My dad will hear of this," he replied, his fists balled at his sides.

His indignation didn't quite make up for the fear that clenched her heart.

3
To Heck with the Consequences

Numbness crawled over J.D.'s skin. His mouth hung open as he watched an officer handcuff Fadwa's mom. The woman complied with her head hanging. Fadwa's dad no longer protested, but the tension in his body made him look like a steel girder ready to snap.

Why are they doing this? Pholatian Protectors were supposed to be... Well, protectors. This didn't make any sense. Since when was it a crime to buy food or a fabricor? Even if they hadn't filed the right paperwork, the punishment shouldn't be this harsh. And the corporal with the frog-like mouth shouldn't take so much joy in harassing these people. Where were the kind officers who went out of their way to be helpful?

Fadwa's sniffles penetrated his stunned state. He stepped closer to her and whispered in her ear. "I'll talk to my dad. Maybe he'll let you stay with us instead. And he can help you."

She kept her gaze fixed on her parents and nodded. "It's untrue. What they speak." Her voice cracked. "My father saved up for the fabricor. It's what I wanted you to view." She wiped her nose. "This has much unfairness. We much need it."

J.D.'s stomach knotted. He'd noticed how skinny she and her family were and understood how a nano-based fabricor would be beneficial for life in space. They couldn't grow a garden as easily as his own mother could. Hunting wasn't an option either.

He wanted to grasp her hand, but her arms were wrapped around her middle as though someone had punched her. His mind sought another way to comfort her.

He inched a little closer, intending to put his arm over her shoulder, but froze midway when Sergeant Vargo arrived with more protectors. His heart jumped. He'd already told the corporal who he was, but seeing the man made him realize just how much trouble he'd soon be in.

Maybe he'll forget I was here. He glanced about, wondering if he could slip away.

One look at Fadwa kept him rooted in place. He couldn't leave her. *To heck with the consequences*. Besides, the sergeant might help straighten this out.

The corporal approached Vargo. He clasped his hands behind him, only releasing them to thumb over his shoulder. The sergeant's eyes snapped J.D.'s way. Then he dipped his head at the corporal and marched over.

J.D.'s heart pulsed in his throat. He swallowed his trepidation and prepared to argue for his friends. Fadwa sucked in a breath and stepped back at the large man's approach. J.D. filled his lungs and straightened, hoping to convey confidence.

Vargo peered down at him with no change in his expression. "Mister Hapker. What are you doing here?"

J.D.'s words caught in his throat. He cleared it, trying to remember what he'd intended to say. "This is my friend, Fadwa." His voice squeaked at the end. "She was showing me her ship when the officers came."

"Your friend? Does your dad know you're out here? The Medberian Plain is no place for a child."

J.D. bristled. He was almost a teenager.

Fadwa's sniffles reminded him that his annoyance was nothing compared to her distress. "There's been a mistake. These people only wanted food and a fabricor."

"They broke the law."

"I'm sure they didn't do it on purpose. Can't you just give them a warning?" J.D. asked in a pleading voice.

"I'm afraid not."

"But why?"

The sergeant's jaw twitched. J.D. got the sense that he didn't like to be questioned. But the man no doubt wanted to avoid offending a legislator's son. "Outsiders tend to skirt the law, regardless of who else it hurts, so we handle them differently."

"Who did they hurt? They just want food."

"Breaking the law affects everyone. Even if unintentional, we must be strict to deter others from trying to lie and steal."

"But she'll be alone, without her family." J.D.'s voice flipped into another high pitch.

"They should have thought about that before they broke the law," Sergeant Vargo said with no hint of remorse.

Fadwa planted herself beside J.D. with clenched fists. "My father is not a lawbreaker! He followed all your regulations!"

Tears threatened to escape her eyes, making J.D.'s sinuses burn. "There must be something we can do," he replied. "You can't send her to one of those horrible detention camps.

"I told you," the corporal interjected, "they're not that bad."

"A child died there!" Heat flushed over J.D.'s face. Neglect, the news had said. His dad had dismissed it too. *Isolated incident.* But rumors had circulated. He'd learned the juvenile detention center wasn't like the childcare centers provided for Pholatians. It was crowded with foreigners who'd been separated from their parents in much the same way Fadwa was about to be. Supervision was inadequate. Sicknesses or injuries got overlooked. Then there was the abuse. The stories he'd heard about what some of the older kids did to the younger ones made his stomach roll.

Sergeant Vargo hesitated, lending truth to the rumors. "Sorry, but the decision has already been made."

J.D. grasped her hand. "She's coming with me."

The sergeant's brow lifted. "That's not how this works."

J.D. remained firm. "She can stay with me and my family."

Vargo harrumphed. "I very much doubt your dad will allow her kind into his home."

Her kind? What the heck was that supposed to mean? She was just a girl. "He will. He's a lot nicer than you," he replied defiantly.

The sergeant scoffed. "Fine. You come along too. I'll call your dad, then you'll see."

Doubt wriggled through J.D.'s insides but he kept a confident expression. Vargo had to be wrong. Although his dad had said some unkind things about the foreigners from the Medberian Plain, he'd change his mind once he met Fadwa.

He will. I just know it.

4

Disillusionment

A tempest of fury and gloom swirled in J.D.'s head while the protectors in the front seat of the vehicle chatted away. They acted as though arresting outsiders was righteous. The navigator, who had nothing else to do while the autopilot drove, gestured wildly as he recounted an incident that'd happened at home, causing the other man to break into laughter… And J.D. to curl his fists.

All the while, Fadwa stared out the window. She hadn't spoken since they got inside. Her hands were clasped in her lap with seeming casualness, but he knew better. She must be so terrified. He certainly would be in her place.

At least Zahir had returned before she'd been taken away. J.D. hadn't seen it swoop over but caught Fadwa whispering at the empty space on the vehicle's roof. There was a distortion when the bird took off, hopefully to somewhere safe until this situation was resolved.

The vehicle eased to a stop in front of a brown brick building with few windows. It rose three stories, looming like an unyielding sentinel and casting an imposing shadow. The wide double-doored entrance reflected like a mirror, preventing him from viewing the fate lurking within.

The blocky lettering naming the building should've given him hope. But instead of spelling *Savyon Peace Station*, the lighting of several letters had gone out, making it read *Sav ace Station*. All someone needed to do was change the c to a g and it'd say *Savage Station*.

He wondered if they'd left it broken on purpose. It'd been evident that they didn't think too highly of the foreigners.

He exited as soon as the doors unlocked and offered Fadwa his hand. She emerged more slowly, her eyes darting about. She shivered and he realized how nippy the night air had turned. If he'd thought to bring his jacket, he would've given it to her. She looked so timid and frail, nothing like the spirited girl he'd met a little over a week ago.

Another vehicle pulled up and parked beside them. Sergeant Vargo stepped out with a blank yet still hard expression. He dismissed the two protectors with a dip of his head.

J.D. glowered as the men marched across the parking lot toward the van holding Fadwa's family. Instead of going through the front doors, the officers escorted them to a brightly lit side entrance. As a biometric authenticator scanned one protector, the others maneuvered the prisoners into the spotlight where another scanner undoubtedly rechecked them for weapons.

Fadwa's parents tolerated the injustice with a tilt of their chins. The door opened and the protectors took them inside. Her dad cast a worried glance over his shoulder before he disappeared.

Fadwa stifled a sob. He squeezed her hand. "It'll be alright," he said, unsure if he still believed it.

"Many thanks for helping," she mumbled.

"Ahem," Sergeant Vargo interrupted. "Let's go."

As he led them to the front doors, Fadwa's eyes widened. "Where do we go?"

"Through the main entrance, for now," Vargo said. "Then someone will drive you to the detention center."

J.D.'s gut twisted. Pholatians rarely got arrested. The pride of Pholatia was that there were more rehabilitative ways to deal with crime than to lock people away. He cringed at the thought of foreigners being jailed often enough that a kid jail was needed.

They entered the main lobby. Dark tiles circled the round space, almost blending in with the cobalt blue walls and heavy black doors. There were five doors in all—one ahead, and two on either side, each with a biometric panel on the right. Benches were interspersed between them.

J.D. had been in peace stations before, and they were usually well-lit and bustling with activity. This depressing place was empty except for the lone officer at the center service window. The white-haired man with a dour expression waited behind an energy shield and what was probably projectile-protective glass. He dipped his head in greeting as Vargo approached, then pressed the intercom. "Legislator Hapker will be here shortly."

J.D.'s chest tightened. Although he didn't care if he got punished, facing his dad's anger and disappointment tapered his earlier storm cloud into guilt.

Everything was so messed up. He'd never told such a big lie before. His parents were likely to ground him for life. No more hanging out with his friends. No trip to the Chenier Islands. He'd have to wait until he was an adult to meet a dragon. The only thing that'd make all this worth it would be if his dad let Fadwa stay with them until her parents were released. The more he thought about his enormous transgression, the less likely this seemed.

Sure enough, when his dad emerged from the right corner door, the air crackled with fury. Legislator Shaul Hapker's long face could be steely when arguing his political standpoints. Now it was harder than J.D. had ever seen it. So hard that the corners of his mouth were white.

J.D. swallowed. His dad should direct most of his ire at those who had mistreated Fadwa's family, but it was all on him. He braced himself as the man approached. "Dad... I'm sorry."

"Let's go, son," he replied, his tone booming like a hammer to stone.

"Wait!" J.D. swiveled toward Fadwa. "She needs someplace to stay."

"We have a place for her."

"You mean the detention center?" he asked, not meaning to sound whiny. "She can't go there."

"When parents break the law, this is the unfortunate consequence for their children." His dad pivoted on his heel, his white legislator's gown swishing around his calves. "Now let's go."

J.D. remained rooted beside Fadwa. "But it's not her fault."

His dad turned with his face scrunched in disgust. "The people who take on this type of lifestyle tend to be riddled with criminality. We can't risk them in the general population."

J.D. pulled back. What was wrong with Fadwa and her family? So what if they lived in space. "Just because you think Pholatians are better doesn't mean we should treat others like they're less."

"You sound like a Cosmopolitan." His dad spit out the name of his rival party as though it were the embodiment of evil.

J.D. remained firm. "Isn't it the philosophy of both the Autarks and the Cosmopolitans to use kindness and understanding to guide people?"

"Our methods may seem harsh to you, but these are the precautions we take to protect our society."

"But why not use compassion?"

Exasperation laced through his dad's groan. "I don't have time to explain this. You will understand when you're older."

J.D. fumed. He hated it when adults told him this. He wasn't stupid. Meanness was usually frowned upon in his family. Having a double standard against those who weren't Pholatian contradicted everything he'd had been taught. The pride he'd once felt for his dad shattered with disillusionment.

"We're leaving now, son," his dad said in that deep, firm tone that brooked no argument.

J.D. hung his head, peeking apologetically at Fadwa whose arms crossed over her stomach. Her eyes glittered with tears. He swallowed the lump in his throat and trudged after his dad.

5
Alone

The air cooled, leaving Fadwa as lonesome as a rogue planet. She clenched her teeth to keep from crying as J.D. deserted her. Despite his slumped shoulders and hanging head, it still felt like a betrayal. At the threshold of the exit, they locked eyes. His crooked frown deepened with forlorn. He mouthed something and this time she read his words… *I won't give up.*

Her father had made the same expression. She used that to stifle her tears. Neither J.D. nor her parents could help her, but she wasn't about to act like a crybaby in front of this officer. Besides, Saba and her dad had always stood tall. She would do the same. She pulled back her shoulders and faced the blond bearded man. "I will go to jail now."

The man's mouth quirked. "You're not going to jail. It's just a place to stay for a bit."

"I can leave it when I want?"

"I'm afraid not."

She scowled. "Then how is it not a jail?"

His replying sigh suggested he didn't have an answer.

"Did J.D. speak true about that child?" she pressed, hoping he'd refute it.

"It…" His throat bobbed. "It was a singular event. Authorities are investigating the matter and working hard to make sure it doesn't happen again."

His tone lacked certainty, exacerbating her trepidation. A tear escaped and trickled down her cheek. "What will I wear?"

His brows curled, then rose in understanding. "We can return to your ship so you can get some clothes."

"Can I get my other things?" she asked hopefully.

He rubbed his bearded chin. She tilted her eyes the way she did when wanting her father to buy her something. He planted his hands on his hips and studied her. "Just a few items," he finally said. "Nothing of value. Theft happens sometimes."

That sounded ominous, but getting to have some of her belongings offered a smidgen of solace.

The officer led her outside and to his vehicle. This one was much the same as the one she'd arrived in—white, boxy, and thickly armored. A string of blue Pholatian letters ran across both the front and back doors. If not for the smaller text underneath it in the Universal Language, she wouldn't have known it said *Pholatian Protection Unit.*

She climbed into the backseat. The door shut, then locked her in like a criminal. The odor here was cleaner than in the other vehicle, but still stuffy. It triggered a claustrophobic sensation—unusual considering the tight quarters she lived in. At least her ship was full of life.

Loneliness surrounded her the entire ride. Her insides twisted in a frenzy as she imagined the isolation that awaited her. She kept telling herself J.D. would come through for her, but her brain wasn't fooled. Not that she lacked faith in her friend—just the system.

They arrived. Seeing her ship closed up and dark sent a pang through her gut. Never had it looked so junky as it did now.

The officer opened her door. She got out, keeping her shoulders straight in false confidence. No way would she let this man see her defeat.

Heading to her home should've eased her distress, but her steps were heavy. When the biometric reader triggered open the hatch, a pang expanded in her chest. The inside lights came on. She expected that seeing her things would cheer her up. But the sharp silence of the empty ship set her teeth on edge. No boisterous laughter from Aymen. No joyful humming from Saba. No patient instruction from her father. It was as though someone had taken a ladle and scooped out the ship's soul.

"I'll wait outside," the officer said. "Get only what you need. I'll check everything over before we go, so no weapons."

Weapons? She might be a space rat, but not a thug. Neither she nor her family would ever hurt anyone. Yeah, her dad had a phaser, but he'd only threatened someone with it that one time docked at Arlentan when a man had snuck onto the ship and pocketed a few things. Even if the thieves here on Pholatia acted in the name of the law, she'd never touch a weapon. *Stupid bigheaded planetsider*.

She meandered through the packed cargo hold, which doubled as a supply room. Items in crates, boxes, and bins were strapped to the walls and floor: tools, assorted spare parts, sealed protein packets, genetically modified seeds, and drums of coffee beans purchased from Dovia that her father would sell for a premium price at the next space station. She hoped they wouldn't spoil while her family languished in jail.

Another item caught her eye. The nano-fabricor was still here. The authorities hadn't taken it yet. She eyed the chrome box. It didn't look like much, but only because it was a modification piece that would attach to their current food processor. The nanoscale robots in this machine converted the simplest of molecules into a variety of complex organic compounds with far more nutritional value. Saba could finally beat her borderline anemia.

The pit of her stomach hardened at the thought of losing it. It wasn't fair.

A blurry shape swept in and landed on the device. Zahir materialized. Fadwa's heart lifted, but only a tad. What would come of him while she was away? He could take care of himself, but he'd be in serious trouble if someone discovered his cybernetics.

She put her finger to her lips. "Be careful," she whispered.

"Be invisible," the bird replied in a lower volume.

"Yes. Be invisible. And be invisible for a long while. I must go."

"Don't go."

"I have no choice."

"Always choices. Zahir help." The bird stared at her, shifting from one foot to the other, waiting.

She cocked her head, considering. The device was too big to carry but could be hauled. It was about a half meter in length and a quarter to a third in width and height. It might fit into her clothes bin, maybe have just enough space left over for her actual belongings.

An idea budded. The invisible weight on her shoulders dwindled, leaving her with newfound energy. It'd be tricky to pull off, but her family couldn't lose this.

She retrieved a roll cart from the storage locker. With much more bounce in her steps than before, she headed into the cabin.

21

The first area was the largest. Part kitchen, part gym, part lounge, it had just enough room for her entire crew to hang out. With no one besides herself in it now, it felt as open and as empty as space.

Gloom fell over her once more. With a clench of her teeth, she bolstered her determination. She marched through, passing their cramped bathroom and each of their somewhat larger bedrooms. She came to the last one on the right and hesitated. Not only would she not see this place again for some time, but she'd also be taking her first step toward open defiance.

Her family was always careful about following the laws of all the places they visited. It was their pride to be different from the sneakthieves and pirates that other traders were known as. If she followed through with her plan, she'd be the first. *What will Father think?*

To hell with these bigheaded planetsiders. *They* were the thieves. She'd only be taking what already belonged to her—well, to her family. But still. She had more of a right to it than the officers did.

She filled her lungs and opened her door. Her first step into lawlessness was also her first step toward righteousness.

6
Squeaky Wheel

The tightness in Fadwa's chest made it difficult to breathe. This was a mistake. What if her crime got her family in more trouble? Father would be cross when he learned she'd defied the law. If he had to suffer for it too, he'd be even more upset. She'd rather eat a bowl of mashed larvae for the rest of her life than face his disappointment.

She glanced down at the roll cart. The fabricor fit perfectly into her bin. She also had room on one side for several protein packets, vacuum-sealed foodstuffs, water bulbs, a flashlight, a battery pack, her father's currency band, and a multi-tool. Her kurtas, leggings, and underclothes were stuffed there too, along with a thermal blanket. The total height of her load was about half a meter. She wished it were shorter, but it would have to do. With any luck, she and the cart would slide right under the space between the rear landing struts and the propulsion units. And with more luck, the bulky Pholatian officer would have a harder time getting through.

It was a good plan, but dare she try it? If she didn't take the fabricor, the authorities would. She clenched her fists and pulled the metal handle of the roll cart. Saving her family's health and livelihood was more important than her honor.

Some spaces were tight as she maneuvered around crates and such. Easier paths were available, but she'd be exposed. Getting as close to the exit as possible without him noticing her offered more of an advantage.

The officer stood outside, a couple meters from the edge of the gate, his head swiveling from side to side as he scrutinized the passersby. With his concern more focused on thieves coming in than her sneaking out, her distress lessened.

As she eased toward the exit, her tension returned. Every squeak of the tires sent her nerves twitching. The officer's attention remained outward even as she reached the bulkhead. She lingered there, hiding behind the jamb. The man was too close. No way would she get down the gangway without him hearing. She needed a distraction.

She considered sending Zahir out but didn't want to risk him being seen. Pholatia was strict about visiting cyborgs. They would undoubtedly put him in a cage.

"Stay invisible," she whispered to the bird perched on her shoulder. Zahir rubbed his head to hers in reply.

Watching the officer watch others gave her an idea. While he distrusted everyone, she knew these people. Sure, several engaged in disreputable practices, but they still tended to look out for one another—especially when dealing with law enforcement. They weren't likely to fight this man for her, but they'd give her a fighting chance.

Two men sauntered by—one skinny and smoking a cigarette, the other hefty and chewing on something. She stepped into full view and frantically waved at them. The big man saw her first, his brows drawing down. She tapped her finger to her lips, then pointed at the officer's back. He dipped his head and nudged his friend with his elbow. They stopped. Their whispers reached her sensitive ears but she didn't understand their language. The skinny man's eyes roved, stopping on her for only half a heartbeat. He dropped his cigarette and ground it with the toe of his boot. Then they approached the officer with a casual gait.

The officer stiffened even more, and she imagined him greeting them with a scowl. With his attention diverted, she tugged on her cart and carefully led it down the gangway. She gritted her teeth at the squeaking wheels, wishing she'd taken the time to grease them.

She stopped near the edge of the gangway. "Whew," she whispered. *Not much more to go.*

The skinny man jabbered, his hands gesturing in wide sweeps. Although she heard their conversation, she paid it no mind. All that mattered was that they keep the officer's attention.

Her insides warmed with gratitude as she eased the roll cart behind her. The clunk of the first set of wheels hitting the gravel made her heart skip a beat. Only the hefty man seemed to notice, but he didn't give her away.

Preventing the wheels from squealing was impossible as she led the cart down the rest of the way. Although she'd tried to take it slow, gravity worked against her. The rear wheels banged over the lip of the gangway, sending her heart into a patter.

She froze as the officer shot a glance over his shoulder. Likely assuming she'd merely come back to him, he returned to the men. "Look," he said. "I've got things to do. You need to move on."

Fadwa held her breath as she pulled the wagon toward the rear of her ship. The two men protested. She picked up her pace, her racing heart urging her to go faster.

"Enough!" the officer snapped.

Knowing he'd return his attention to her, she bolted. Somewhere nearby, Zahir belched a warning caw, heightening her panic.

"Hey! Where do you think you're going?"

The officer's footsteps clomped on the hard ground behind her. She ran as fast as her load allowed. Upon reaching the gap under the ship, she yanked the cart in front of her and pushed it under. The space was barely big enough, forcing her to drop to her hands and knees and scrabble through.

Just as she slid under herself, the officer grabbed her ankle. Panic sprang like a leak in a pressurized water line. She jerked her leg. The grip dragged her. Her thigh scraped along the ground. She clutched the side of the landing strut and held on for dear life. The officer was much stronger than her. His elbow bent as he drew her near. The twist of annoyance on his red face ratcheted up her terror. She rolled onto her back, then struck out with her boot. It smacked his wide nose. He bellowed but didn't let go. The hazy shape of Zahir flew at his head. The flapping of wings combined with the bird's cries finally caused the man to release her. She flipped about and scrambled out on her hands and knees, ignoring the sharp rocks cutting into her skin.

Fadwa reached the other side and faced a set of worn shoes. *Uh oh.*

She swallowed and arched her neck. The skinny man stood before her with a smile on his face and his hand held out. She looked at it with askance, then grasped it.

"I wish you luck, little miss," he said in the Universal Language. After a quick salute, he took off at a jog.

She shook herself free of the shock, then dashed in the opposite direction with her cart in tow. The screeching of the wheels sliced through the silence of the night, but at least they were the only sound. No tromping footsteps came after her. No yells either. Did that mean he'd decided not to chase her, or was he taking another route to cut her off?

With the earlier throng thinned, the wide space between parked ships left her exposed. She had to find a place to hide—somewhere that kept all prying eyes away. That certainly wouldn't be the shipyard. Although those two men had helped her, others might not be so accommodating. And some would offer help only to steal her things, and she shouldn't afford to lose the fabricor.

Where to go?

"This way!" Zahir called. She couldn't see him but didn't need to.

Following the sound of his flapping wings, she came upon another ship. It was bigger than hers and appeared to be locked down for the night. Her breath shook as she tiptoed along the side, keeping close. The flat-bellied vessel had landing struts similar to her own, which left a nice little nook when they lowered. Their size promised enough space for both her and the cart to squeeze into. It'd be a good place to hide until morning when the crowd thickened once more. By then, every law enforcement officer would be looking for her, but she'd have a better chance than she had now.

Assuming this ship doesn't leave in the middle of the night. A gruesome image of her being squished by the struts made her cringe, but she didn't have the luxury of options.

With a determined yet still hesitant breath, she ducked under and hoped for the best.

7
Family Squabble

If anger could fuel a fire, J.D. would be spewing it like a dragon. As he stared out the vehicle window with the city passing by in a night-lit blur, his brain kept spinning back to his father's comment about him being too young to understand. At that time, J.D. had felt belittled. Now he grasped the laziness of the reply. If his dad's actions were so right, why couldn't he give a satisfactory explanation?

He suspected adults only said that when they subconsciously knew their line of thinking was flawed. After all, that'd happened to him when his little brother Matz had asked him why he was no longer friends with Ruel. The situation was a mess of insults and hard feelings that revolved around a girl. And although Ruel had started it with his jealous digs, J.D. shouldn't have blown up at him like that. Would he admit it, though? No. Not even to Matz. *"You'll understand when you're older,"* he'd finally told his brother.

J.D. clenched his fists. How could he make a convincing argument when his dad was being stubborn? Maybe he could appeal to his mother. Surely, she would see the injustice in locking up a child's entire family over a food fabricor. If anyone could talk her dad into seeing reason, it was her.

He mapped out all the things he would say. At first, his imagination presented him as calm and reasonable. But his outrage eventually took over and he visualized his argument as a squabble of yelling and insults.

When they reached home. J.D. exited the car, keeping his eyes fixed on his front door and his mouth pinched shut. His dad did the same as J.D. came inside, only his silence pressed down like the giant paw of an annoyed lion.

"Oh," his mom said to him as she wiped the kitchen table. "You're back."

27

"Dad arrested an entire family and sent the girl to a juvenile detention center," J.D. blurted. "All because they bought a food fabricor."

His mom halted mid-wipe and straightened. Her brows drew down the way they always did when given distressing news. "That's awful. Why would they put her there?"

"Because she's not Pholatian."

"Oh." Her tone implied no concern as she resumed cleaning.

J.D.'s jaw dropped. So treating other people like they were less just because they weren't from the same planet didn't bother her either? *That's so warped!*

His dad entered and smacked his work tablet on the table. "Turns out J.D. wasn't camping with his friends," he thundered. "He went to the Medberian Plain."

This time, his mom's shock was more pronounced. Her hands flew to her cheeks, her mouth fell open, and a gasp escaped her. "He did what?"

The loudness of her voice nearly matched his dad's. J.D.'s words locked in his throat as blood surged to his head, making him dizzy. This couldn't be happening. Since when had his mistakes been more concerning than injustice?

"At night!" his dad raged on. "He got caught hanging out with a bunch of criminals."

J.D. tensed at how his dad made it sound like he'd been committing a crime. No wonder his mom looked so pale. "Criminals?" she asked.

"That's right. Criminals." A cord in his dad's neck bulged as he yelled. "The protectors had arrested these thugs for trying to steal a fabricor and guess who they found with him?" He jabbed his finger at J.D. "Our son! Hanging out with the dregs of the galaxy. He's lucky he didn't get himself killed!"

J.D. tensed as he tried to process the situation. His dad had never hidden his aversion toward non-Pholatians, but the level of hatefulness spewing from him now was beyond belief. It was like he was a whole different person. J.D.'s throat finally unlocked and words zipped out like angry bees. "That's not how it happened! I was with a friend. No laws were being broken."

"They had no right to that fabricor!" His dad said, hands on hips and looming over him with fury blazed in his eyes.

"They got a permit to buy it," J.D. replied, trying to match his dad's outrage.

"That seems highly unlikely. These people are nothing but thieves and liars!"

"How do you know?"

"Because I do, darn it! It's how they operate. They're not like us. Not only did you create a situation that'll potentially affect my chances of reelection—"

J.D. clenched his teeth. Of course this was about how everything reflected on him and his political career.

"—you also put yourself in danger!" his dad continued. "What if they hurt you? Or worse? Killed you?"

Fadwa would never hurt him, and he doubted her family would either. "You don't know them."

"And I don't want to know the likes of them!"

J.D. stamped his foot. "They didn't do anything wrong! All they wanted was a fabricor so they could eat better. How is that illegal?"

His dad threw up his hands. "Basic economics! If they reverse engineer it and make more to spread throughout the galaxy, our agricultural trade will dwindle. People will lose their jobs and our economy will fall into a recession."

J.D. stuck out his bottom lip. Although he understood the economic concepts, he still didn't get why those things were more important than feeding people—especially those who lived in space where food wasn't easy to come by.

He gave up on arguing it. His dad wasn't listening anyway. The only way to win this was for Fadwa's family to be proven innocent. "So if the protectors find they filed the correct paperwork to buy that fabricor, they'll be released?"

His dad scoffed. "Yes, but they won't get to keep the thing. By the time they're let out, it will be illegal for them to have it."

"What? Why?"

"I just told you why!" His dad threw up his hands. "Did you not hear a word I said?"

J.D. faced his mom. "I'm sorry I went there, alright. Ground me for a year—for life! But a girl my age is in a kid jail where another child recently died," he implored. "You can't do that to her. Let her stay with us until her family is proven—"

Dawn Ross

"Absolutely not!" his dad interrupted. "We're not letting trash stay at our house."

J.D. gave his mom his best pleading expression. Her lips pressed into a thin line. "Your dad is right. We don't know these people. Who knows what kind of person this girl is? What if she steals our things? What if she hurts you? Or your brother?" She wagged her head. "I won't allow it."

J.D.'s shoulders fell. Everyone was against him—against Fadwa and her family. He had no hope of winning an argument against adults, no matter how righteous. When his dad ordered him to his room, he obeyed. If he were an omega dog, his ears would be laid back, his head would hang low, and his tail would be tucked between his legs.

Poor Fadwa. He hoped the detention center wasn't as bad as everyone claimed.

As he plopped on his bed, his hands clasped behind his head, his mind searched for other ways he could help his friend.

"J.D." a small voice said. Matz hovered at the edge of his door, his straight sandy hair sticking out in more places than usual, and his forehead wrinkled. "Dad's really mad."

"Yeah," J.D. replied, not sure how to explain the situation to a nine-year-old.

"What happened?"

J.D. exhaled slowly. "I told Dad I was camping, but I wasn't. I was with a friend."

Matz's little mouth formed into a circle. "Woah. You're gonna be grounded forever, aren't you?"

"Probably," J.D. said, annoyance tainting his tone. "Now go back to bed or you'll get in trouble too."

Their parents seldom yelled, so Matz's stricken expression made sense as he hurried to his room.

J.D. lay in near silence as his dad's muffled voice rumbled below. Every now and then, the voices rose. They invariably calmed, though. Mom occasionally debated things with his dad but never outright contradicted him—never. He should've known. His dad was too hard-headed, always insisting he was right even when he was wrong, and his mom was too agreeable to press the issue.

The house comm rang, startling him into an upright position. No one called here this late unless it was important.

30

His heart ticked up a notch. Maybe the authorities were calling to say Fadwa's family had been innocent. That would be fitting.

He tiptoed to his door and held his breath.

"Hello?" his dad said.

"Sorry to bother you at this hour, Legislator Hapker," a woman replied.

J.D. almost whooped. It was Gayleen, his father's aide, and her voice carried a hint of *you're-not-going-to-like-this*. Even better, the comm was on speaker, allowing him to hear both sides of the conversation.

He grinned at the prospect of Fadwa and her family being set free—and at his dad being proven wrong.

8

Runaway

Fadwa eyed the dwindling gap behind the landing strut and frowned. It turned out the cart was too long to get all the way in. She could have forced it but that would've made too much noise. The bin with the fabricor fit well enough, but there was little room left for her unless she wanted to twist herself into a painfully tight knot.

She rubbed her eyes as an ache built up behind them. Her brain worked like an overtaxed engine, losing the fight against her exhaustion.

Resting wasn't an option. Three times now, Zahir had warned her of patrolling officers. All places like this had a fair amount of security, but Pholatian Protectors took their jobs far too seriously. Was this because of her? Surely taking what belonged to her family shouldn't attract this much attention.

She evaluated the hiding space once more and groaned. This wouldn't work. She had to find another place. But where?

Along the sunrise side of the shipyard lay a town of sorts. At its center were dozens of buildings dedicated to running the spaceport. Supporting businesses and shops fanned out from either side. Port Town contained mostly service centers, supply stores, and a few small-scale factories. Her father had said that even though some businesses were open all night, many of the transactions that took place during that time were illegal. It probably wasn't a good idea to go there.

But Starboard Town was even more dangerous. It was more of a ramshackle trading post than an organized town. People went there to trade a variety of goods. They also liked to visit the area's taverns and entertainment clubs. It was barely a safe place for a young girl with her father during daylight hours. Going at night would get her in more trouble than being found by the Pholatian Protectors.

She considered staying here. So far none of the officers had thought to look under the ships, but it was only a matter of time. All it would take was one officer to duck down.

Port Town, then. The service centers tended to pile their broken junk around their buildings, making some great hiding places. And if she stayed away from the inner parts of town, she had a good chance of staying clear of criminal activity. The hardest part would be avoiding the patrols.

She grabbed her things and set them back on the roll cart. Getting the bin with the fabricor required a noisy struggle, but she did it without attracting trouble.

With everything ready, she crawled under the lower sections of the ship to avoid exposing herself. The clicking of Zahir's beak made her halt. The bird perched somewhere above her, keeping a lookout. Earlier he'd cawed out of instinct. Now he was being consciously cautious, communicating with a series of clicks that only she'd detect.

She ducked further into the shadows. A few meters away, the old and tattered shoes of an enviro-suit shuffled by. She waited until the night went silent again before poking her head out.

The area was clear. She braced herself, then stepped out. Her heart leapt to her throat as she darted across the way. The ear-splitting squeal of her cart's wheels seemed loud in the oppressive night. She imagined everyone within a ten-kilometer radius hearing them.

She made it to another ship. Its low thruster gave her new cover. She hugged the ship's hull, panting and willing her panic down. When her racing heart eased somewhat, she signaled to Zahir. The bird emitted a series of clicks, telling her two officers approached from the left. She risked a peek, then squeaked like a rodent stowaway and scuttled further under the thruster. They were far enough away that they hadn't noticed her in the darkness, but they were moving closer. With no other options available, she held her breath and waited.

The internal thudding in her ears masked the sound of the bootsteps, making it difficult to tell how close they were. She willed her heart to calm, but thinking about it only made it thump harder.

Zahir clicked, telling her they headed away now. She glanced out to confirm, catching their profiles as they turned down an intersection. She puffed. *That was close.*

She rushed to another ship, avoiding the spotlights that dotted the area. The next vessel was further than the others, but she made it without being seen. Port Town was within her sights, but its streetlights were so far that they might as well be distant galaxies. This was a horrible idea. Hopping from ship to ship would take her all night. There had to be a better way that wouldn't leave her exposed.

A growing vibration grew to the rumbling of a choking engine. Zahir clicked to confirm the approach of a man in a vehicle. She tensed and peeked out. Two lights, one dimmer than the other, drew near. A spotlight illuminated a rusted and battered transport. Not a patrol car. The tightness of her gut eased.

As it lumbered closer, the next lamppost revealed the driver. From this distance, the man resembled the hefty one who had helped her earlier. It gave her an idea.

She stepped out. The man's brows drew down. He slowed down, his vehicle stuttering to a stop beside her. "You alright, miss?" the man asked, leaning partway out the open cab window.

She regarded the mini car. The cab was just barely big enough for him to sit, making him look like an animal crammed into a cage. The car's longish bed was fenced in with wood, of all things, but covered with a tarp. She couldn't tell how much it held but hoped there'd be room for her. "I need a ride to Port Town. Can you help me?"

His mouth quirked into a half smile. "Whatcha doing?" he asked in the Universal Language. "Running away?"

"No," she blurted, hoping he didn't see through the lie. "I must convey this to my father." She indicated her roll cart with a wave of her hand.

His eyes roved over her and the cart. She shifted her feet and prayed he'd honestly try to help. An uneasy feeling fell over her, like she'd jumped out of the path of an oncoming ship only to get blasted by its radioactive emissions.

The man got out, making her step back even though he didn't approach her. Instead, he ambled with a slight limp to the rear and opened the tailgate. A section of the gate flipped out, creating a

34

steepish ramp. "I got a bit of room in the trailer for both you and your things. It ain't much, but it'll get you to Port Town."

She veered her cart around him in an arc wide enough to be out of his reach, but close enough to not appear rude. The bed was only half full, but it would still be a tight fit.

As though sensing her wariness, he stepped back and motioned for her to get in. "Pull the gate up after you. It'll click shut. Keep the tarp over you, if you would. I don't want no one knowing what I got in here," he said with a wink.

Yeah, he knew she was running away from something. Not good. But she rolled her cart up and pushed it in. It was too long, so she maneuvered it sideways, then squeezed in beside it. After pulling up the tailgate, she grabbed a corner of the tarp and yanked it over her. A plop and crinkle signified Zahir had perched above.

The vehicle choked back to life. She hunched over and kept her balance by hugging the fabricor. The ride jounced her around, but it was better than running and ducking into tiny places while hauling a heavy cart.

Minutes passed. She glimpsed several ships through the wooden slats. She should be almost there. The fluttering in her stomach intensified. Impatience got the best of her. She lifted a corner of the tarp.

A rock-strewn ledge towered over, making her heart stop. This was at the opposite end of the spaceport. Where was this man taking her?

The revelation shocked her into action. She scrambled for the gate latch. Finding it on the outside, she curled her fingers under it and jerked up. The tailgate clattered open. The vehicle slowed. She maneuvered the cart with a jerk and leapt out.

Her momentum threw her on the ground, skinning her knees. The cart crashed into her, cutting into her ankle.

The vehicle lurched to a stop and the door flew open. "Hey! What are ya doing?"

She scrambled to her feet, grabbed the cart's handle, and ran as fast as her legs cold carry her. Her knees and ankle throbbed, but the adrenaline zipping through her numbed the pain. Her cart squealed like a mouse caught in a trap.

"Get back here, you urchin!" the man bellowed.

Her ragged breaths couldn't pull in enough air. Her body tingled as she hastened along the base of the scree. She risked a glance over her shoulder. He pursued but waddled with a limp that was much worse than what she'd noted before.

Her energy flagged. He yelled more insults. His voice seemed more distant so she took another peek. Sure enough, he'd fallen farther behind. Her limbs threatened to give out with relief, but she pressed on. No doubt he'd get back in his vehicle and follow in that, so she had to climb.

A space between two giant boulders allowed her to roll her cart in and hide. Ducking low even though the rocks were taller than her father, she weaved and climbed where possible. No way would she be able to haul the cart to the top. She had to camouflage it, then abandon it—at least for a while.

She eyed the rim of the cliff and hoped J.D. was up there, keeping his promise to help her. Maybe he was on the ledge right now waiting for her.

"Zahir? Zahir!" she whispered. The bird landed on her shoulder. "Check for J.D. up there."

"Danger. Won't leave," he said in a low volume.

"Please. Possibly he can give aid."

"Go look. Keep watch." Zahir flew off.

She waited. An engine growled near. She tucked in and tried to rein in her panting. The clouds above reflected light from the towns across and the sprawling city above, leaving her in a forest of shadows. That man would have to climb with his gimpy leg. Unless he saw where she'd gone, he'd have trouble finding her. At least she hoped so.

The crunching of rubber on gravel got louder. She squeezed her eyes shut. Some people in the galaxy prayed, but she'd never understood the purpose until now. Not knowing which god to speak to, she murmured a general plea for help from anyone who had the heart to listen to a space rat.

The crackles stopped and the vehicle's engine silenced. Her chest constricted. She strained her ears, hoping not to hear footsteps. Only the bugs that J.D. had called sand grylli made noise. Any other time, their rhythmic trilling would have comforted her. Now she worried they masked the movements of her hunter.

A spurting clamor erupted as the car's engine came back to life. The popping of the gravel resumed. She dared not celebrate just yet. Her body cramped, willing her to move but she remained still. Dizziness threatened to overcome her. She gripped the rough edge of a rock and lent it some of her weight.

The sound eventually faded from range. With a long sigh, she rose on shaky legs. Arching her neck, she gazed at the starry sky. "Many thanks to you."

9
Political Standpoint

Shaul Hapker paced from his dining area to the living room and back. His steps created muffled thumps on the lush carpet. His thoughts spun with all the possible scenarios that could erupt from his son's stupidity. *What a disaster!* What the hell had J.D. been thinking? He'd told him to stay away from that place.

Dina put a hand on his forearm. The green flecks of her hazel eyes were soft with sympathy. How could she be so calm? But that was one reason he loved her so much. She was the eye of his sometimes-stormy spirit. Politics could be a bear, but she had a way of helping him keep a cool head.

Even now his temper settled, though it didn't go away. No chance of that anytime soon. "He is grounded for…" He flicked his hand. "Eternity."

"Well, yes. He's certainly grounded. What was he doing out there, exactly?"

"Hell if I know." He rubbed his temples, trying to piece together the details.

"Perhaps we should ask him when we're all calm. There must be a logical reason for it."

He harrumphed. "I'm not sure what difference it makes. The fact is that he lied to us. He was supposed to be camping."

She sighed and eased down onto the couch, pulling him beside her. "That just doesn't sound like him."

Shaul patted her hand. Poor Dina. As caring as she was, she could never believe ill of anyone. Her geniality made her a great politician's wife. It also made her a bit gullible. Thank goodness his savvy balanced it out.

"Legislator Gozal is going to have a field day when he finds out my son was caught hanging out with criminals."

Delicate furrows formed between Dina's brows. A loose lock of light blond hair fell over it. "Doesn't he empathize with the outsiders? He's a Cosmopolitan after all."

It didn't happen often, but sometimes she made a decent point. If Gozal found out people claiming to have filed the correct paperwork for a nano-machine had been arrested, he'd raise a fuss.

"Darned Cosmopolitans. Spreading our ideals to the galaxy sounds good for the galaxy, but what about the good of Pholatia?" He shook his head with an annoyed huff. "We have something special here. A society with little crime and virtually no violence. These outsiders threaten that. Did you know our spaceports have more crime in one week than our capital city has in an entire year? It's unacceptable."

"But those crimes are confined to the spaceport. How do they influence our society?"

"The spaceport doesn't operate in a bubble, dear." He patted her hand. "Our people interact with those people. And the more interaction, the greater the possibility of contamination. Do you remember that atrocious music craze with the ear-splitting instruments and the screaming of the lyrics? That nastiness didn't develop in Pholatia. And that's just music. You don't even want to know about the entertainment bots that've been smuggled in."

His party, the Autarks, had the right of it. Preserve their culture by limiting galactic commerce. That was the belief Pholatia had been founded on all those centuries ago. It was why much of their natural habitats were still intact, and why they remained mostly agrarian.

"We honestly don't need outsiders here at all," he continued. "If it were up to me, I wouldn't allow anyone to come here. But one step at a time."

The priority was to keep Gozal from finding out and turning this into a pity-fest for those dregs. The next important thing was to outlaw the export of those nano-machines. But that would be taken care of soon enough. The bill would be voted on in a week. Its wording would also allow for ones purchased beforehand to be confiscated, but only if they hadn't left the planet yet.

He sighed. If Gozal used his son's actions against him, he could lose the majority vote. Heck, it might even keep him from getting reelected! Darn boy. What was he thinking?

The house comm rang, making him snap upright. *Oh hell.* The political upheaval was already starting.

Shaul rose with moderate haste and answered. "Hello?"

"Sorry to bother you so late, Legislator Hapker," his aide said.

"It's alright, Gayleen. What's going on?"

"It's about the girl."

Shaul's mouth twisted. "What of her?"

"The sergeant in charge escorted her back to her ship to get some clothes. She grabbed the nano-fabricor instead and took off."

Shaul's blood pressure spiked. "Took off how?"

"On foot, apparently—with the fabricor in a handcart."

"How in the heck did she outrun a Pholatian officer?"

"The sergeant said he was distracted."

"Distracted?" Shaul shrieked. "How?"

"Two outsiders asked him a bunch of questions while the girl snuck off."

"That sounds intentional." *Darned foreigners.* Pholatia's crime rates would be near zero if not for these spaceports and their lowlife cargo crews.

"I believe it was. You know how those types stick up for one another."

"I hope they've been arrested."

"Unfortunately, they also disappeared."

"Well, hell." Shaul kicked at a nonexistent object. "Make sure that sergeant is written up."

"Already on it. There's more, Senator."

Shaul heaved a sigh. What else could possibly go wrong? "Go on."

"This might actually be helpful. She assaulted the officer during her escape—gave him a bloody nose and cut up his face. We believe she used some sort of tech to do it, too—at least for the cuts."

"That *is* good news. If her family's papers turn out to be legitimate, we can still hold them. Make sure they're held until we find the girl and confiscate the fabricor."

"Will do, Senator."

"I take it you are looking for her?"

"Yes, Sir. No luck, though. I suspect she's found other outsiders to help her. Possibly the same ones who distracted the sergeant."

"See that she's caught, Gayleen. And keep this as far away from Legislator Gozal and his ilk as much as you can."

"We're making all this our top priority."

She disconnected. He plopped back down onto the couch next to Dina and cradled his forehead in his palm.

What a gosh darned stinking mess.

10
Getting Away

A biting wind numbed J.D.'s nose and ears. He pulled on his hood as he pedaled his ecobike down the lit yet still dark neighborhood streets. Since his motor had been emitting a high-pitched whine lately, manual power would have to do until he got to the city proper. Not that he used the electrified momentum much anyway, but he needed to find Fadwa before they captured her. No way would he let her get taken to that horrible detention center now that they'd labeled her a criminal.

It'd been a half hour since he snuck out and his temper still soared. How could his dad do those hateful things? Arresting them before knowing whether they'd done anything illegal was bad enough. Now he was conspiring to keep them longer just to deprive them of the fabricor. It made no sense.

His family had always helped people. Mom donated more than half the food from her garden to those in need. Both his parents attended several charitable functions a year. And at least once a month, J.D. and Matz joined them in a community volunteer project. His dad's reaction toward Fadwa's family just because they weren't Pholatian went against everything they'd taught him.

The first businesses appeared—salons, souvenir shops, restaurants, clothing stores—all closed for the night. He steered clear of the open convenience mart, then turned onto the pathway beside the usually busier Cresthill Street. He risked a Pholatian Protector patrol spotting and interrogating him, but he figured all the darkened office buildings along this route meant fewer patrols than the wider streets or the ones with convenience marts and all-night eateries.

The more he rode and the closer he got to the Medberian Plain, the greater his uncertainty. Would he find her at their usual meeting spot or at her ship? Where would he search if she wasn't at either?

His insides twisted at the thought of her spending the night in some dark place, alone and without a blanket. He'd brought her one, and some clothes too. She'd also need food, but the carbo drink and a bag of snack crisps from his desk were all he could grab.

Both her current and potential suffering had galvanized him into sneak out. What did they expect her to do when faced with having to go to kid jail? Of course she had to get away.

The violence she'd done had shocked him at first, but it made sense. He doubted she'd hurt the officer out of malice. He also didn't think the officer would try to harm her. But she wouldn't have known that. She'd probably reacted out of desperation and terror.

A set of headlights appeared ahead. All the buildings before him connected in a seamless line, forcing him to veer back the way he'd come. He pedaled hard, racing to get to a cross street before the vehicle got close enough to see him.

No luck. The hum of a quiet engine reached his ears before he could turn off. The vehicle drove past. It was a darker color, so not a patrol cruiser. He huffed in relief, then turned back toward the spaceport. This time, he used the ecobike's motor. Its whining grated on his nerves but the sooner he got to this destination, the better.

Twenty minutes later, he glimpsed the twinkling lights of the Medberian Plain. A stretch of tiny shops lined the ledge overlooking the area. This was a tourist spot, after all. Part of what had drawn J.D. here to begin with was all the wares from other parts of the galaxy.

He dismounted his ecobike and wheeled it between two cottage-sized stores. The one on his left sold gold-flecked green jewels from Sendia while the other on the right offered decorative and lightweight stoneware from a planet he couldn't pronounce the name of. They were both closed, of course. As were all the other places here.

The backside of some buildings had built up some clutter. His tires crunched on the gravel as he searched for a place to hide his ecobike. As much as it would benefit him on the plain, hauling it down in the dark seemed like a bad idea.

He found a spot beneath what looked like a pile of packing material. After donning his pack, he headed to the place he'd met Fadwa earlier today. At about half a kilometer away, he was still at risk of getting caught. No doubt Pholatian Protectors patrolled this area too.

The wind blew harder here. It swept in from below, conveying a sour hint of spent fuel. It also carried grit. Pricks of sand splattered his exposed face, adding to the biting cold. Searing hot during the day and freezing at night, it was no wonder the plains had never been cultivated.

A silhouette appeared from the side of a shop designed to look like a hut. J.D. darted between two rectangular buildings and pressed against the wall as best he could with the pack on his back. He slid along the roughened stucco wall. It was probably just a shopkeeper getting ready for the morning, but his blood pumped nonetheless.

He made it to the front edge and peeked around the corner.

"Boo!"

J.D. yowled and lurched away from a broad-faced man with a wicked grin that displayed a missing front tooth. Panic clutched J.D.'s heart like a hawk's talons.

"Whatcha doing out here, boy?"

J.D. spun on his heel and darted toward the other end. Another man appeared. This one larger—and uglier. Wild red hair darkened by the night covered him from the top of his head down to the bushy beard that rested on his round gut. The stench wafting off him was like the puke that vultures spewed when confronted by a predator.

He turned about wildly looking for an escape, but they had him trapped between the buildings.

"Lookie what we got here," the hairy man said. "A local will fetch a good ransom, ya think?"

"What? No!" J.D. screeched.

"You betcha. Just look at 'im," the wide-faced man replied. "Nice clothes. Nice shoes. He's likely got a rich family."

"The Protectors will come after you," J.D. protested, desperation scrabbling under his skin.

"They won't come for you in space, boy."

The palpitations in J.D.'s chest intensified. He darted his eyes about, hoping to find an opening for escape. The wild-haired man was larger, but he'd left a bigger gap on his right side. J.D. took it, diving low and pitching himself around like a deranged squirrel. The man snatched for him, his hands raking across J.D.'s pack, and missed.

J.D. tripped over his own feet and nosedived onto the gravel. He scrambled to rise, but the wild-haired man had him by the hem of his pants while the broad-faced one grabbed his ankle.

Fear wrapped around J.D.'s throat, keeping him from screaming. The men yanked him close and towered over him like hungry jackals. His palms scraped the spiky rocks. The broad-faced man cackled while the other emitted a deep chuckle.

A blur swept in from overhead and smacked the wild-haired man in the face. His shriek and Zahir's angry caw resounded like two fighting falcons.

Something long and black struck the broad-faced man on the side of the head. The clang that sounded revealed the source—a metal pipe being wielded by a small shadow that whirled like a ferocious kitten.

J.D. scrambled to his feet in shock. Fadwa smacked the wild-haired man again as he tried to get up. Zahir harassed the other one, beating with its wings and raking with its talons.

The men scurried back. Fadwa tossed the pipe aside as though it had bitten her. J.D. panted. A mixture of awe, relief, and gratitude bombarded him. She was safe… And she'd just saved his life. Before he could thank her, she grabbed his hand and they sprinted off. His legs threatened to give out beneath him as she led the way. If the men yelled or gave chase, J.D. couldn't tell through the pounding in his eardrums.

They reached their usual meeting place and Fadwa leapt below the ledge with the grace of a fleeing gazelle. He feared his gangly clumsiness but maybe if he stepped where she stepped, he'd be alright.

A clattering of pebbles rolled past him. His vigor renewed as the two men attempted to follow. They didn't yell, probably so as not to attract protectors, but their bumbling made more than enough noise.

His dad might be right about the Medberian Plain being a dangerous place.

He slipped, falling backward. His elbow cracked on a rock and his butt crashed onto a jagged edge. Fadwa stopped. He couldn't see her face, but he imagined her wide eyes. She helped him up and they resumed.

More stones fell. One man grunted, his voice closer.

Dawn Ross

J.D. attempted to pick up his pace but a sharp twang in his hips made maneuvering difficult. Despite the cool night, sweat poured down his face.

An ear-splitting snap cut through the air, followed by a squawk and a pain-filled roar. J.D. darted onward, hoping the noise meant one of them had broken a bone during their descent.

Inspired by the lucky happenstance, J.D. forgot all about his hip and bounded the rest of the way down the slope with Fadwa.

11
Broken Spirit

The night stilled. Even the sand grylli were quiet. The dead calm should have been comforting. It meant they weren't being chased anymore. But recent events had taken their toll. J.D. had never experienced anything close to this level of danger before. Well, there was that time he'd stumbled upon a pair of spire cat cubs at the same moment their mom had returned from a hunt. But at least the animal hadn't acted out of malice.

After finding a well-hidden cranny between the boulders, he removed the thermal blanket from his pack and scooted in beside Fadwa. He wrapped one end around her shoulder and drew the other over himself. The wind didn't reach here but the rocks reflected the coldness of the desert night. Plus his adrenaline had worn off, leaving him with a bone-aching chill. The way she huddled close to him suggested she probably felt it too.

She nestled within the nook of his arm. Her shoulders shook. At first, he thought she was shivering. The rhythm of her movements told him it was something else. "Are you crying?" he asked, anguished at her broken spirit. She sniffled in reply. He tightened his embrace. "It's alright. We're safe. I doubt they're looking for us in the dark."

She wiped her nose with her sleeve. "It's not that."

"Your family." He swallowed down the rising guilt. "I'm sorry about my dad. I've never known him to act this way."

"My father..." More tears fell. "My father will have much disappointment in me."

What? "Why? You *had* to run away. They didn't leave you any choice."

"I hurt that officer. Then I hurt one more person tonight."

"That officer should've left you alone. And you and Zahir saved my life. Your dad will be proud of you."

"You have no comprehension. We aren't lawbreakers and we don't cause harm. My actions oppose our values."

Oh. He related—somewhat. One time when this bratty kid named Ethan was picking on his little brother, J.D. intervened by pushing him down. He must've pushed too hard because Ethan fell back and bumped his head. Next thing he knew, Pholatian Protectors were at his door. It was a huge mess. The way J.D.'s parents looked at him with horror still hurt his stomach. Although they'd ultimately understood, the long lecture he'd received afterward made him realize how important it was to think before you act and only use force as a last resort.

But this was different. "You had no choice," he said firmly. Even his dad had conceded that sometimes force was necessary. "You have a right to protect yourself—and others. I'm sure your dad will understand." *Mine did. Though he's being hateful and stubborn now.*

Fadwa didn't reply, but she seemed calmer.

A blur swept in and Zahir appeared. "Gone. No more bad men."

J.D. slumped. *Thank goodness.* He nudged Fadwa and handed her his pack. "Hey, I brought stuff for you."

"What is it?"

"Food and water. I can bring you more tomorrow."

She gripped his arm. "You will leave me solus?"

"Umm." He hadn't intended to remain with her. But now that he was here, it made sense that she expected him to run away with her. "I-I can't stay. If my dad finds out I'm gone, he'll send the entire force out to look for me."

"Oh." She hung her head. "That has sense. But I can't remain here. The dangers are too great. And your police will locate me."

J.D. agreed. This was a good place to hide at night but anyone up on the ledge would notice her during the day. He wracked his brain, trying to think of a way to protect her. Would one of his dad's political rivals help? Legislator Gozal, perhaps? Maybe, but it wasn't like he had his direct contact information. Besides, what would he even say? *Hey, this is Legislator Hapker's son. I'm calling to see if you'll do me a favor.* Most likely, the man would hang up on him as soon as he heard his family name. Plus J.D. couldn't be sure he'd want to help. And suppose he did, how long would it take? Fadwa needed help now.

"I know where you can go," he said. "The protectors will never think to search for you there either."

"Where?" Fadwa asked, eagerness spiking her tone.

"The Spire Wilderness."

She pulled back. "The wild? I have no comprehension of wild things."

"It's easy. And like I said, I can bring you more food and water."

"I have some. Hidden."

Oh yeah. She'd taken the fabricor too, yet it was nowhere in sight.

"Okay, then. Get it. Then I'll take you to the Spires and show you where to stay. They have caves there. Nothing deep, but enough to hide you."

"What if animals come?"

The spire cats rarely attacked people. But like any predator, they'd take advantage of what they perceived as an easy target, and Fadwa *was* small. "I'll bring you my hunting knife. Make it into a spear."

She didn't reply right away. He bumped shoulders with her. "Hey. It'll be alright. I'll get you to a cave, fortify it a bit, then come back tomorrow to show you what to do."

He didn't tell her how challenging it would be for him to sneak off again. No doubt his parents would keep a closer eye on him. But he'd find a way. He wouldn't leave her to fend for herself.

*****

It was too much. Fadwa wrapped her arms around her head. She'd never been without her family before. Not once. Her life was falling apart. And now she was facing an even more frightening concept—being alone in the wild on a strange planet.

Nothing J.D. said comforted her. All the terrible things that could go wrong weighed on her more than high-Gs. But what choice did she have?

She wiped her eyes. What if she let herself get caught? After all, she'd hidden the fabricor by piling a bunch of rocks over it. No one would know it was there. But what if after they had her, they made her tell where it was? Authorities in other places had been known to

49

be rough with travelers, and she wasn't sure she could withstand the threat of harm, let alone actual violence.

J.D. patted her shoulder. "I won't let you be out there by yourself the whole time. I'll visit as often as I can. You'll be safe. I promise."

"It sounds scary."

"It can be. But think of it this way. While you know the universe, I know the woods. I'll show you all the tricks." The confidence in his voice opened her up to the idea, but she hesitated. "Come on," he added. "It's got to be better than kid jail."

The reminder of the child that had died there made up her mind, but she still had questions. "How do we get there?"

"The skytran runs all night. We can take that."

"What's a skytran?"

"It's a series of long cars that a bunch of people can ride at once."

Like a coach, then. Or a train or magpod. The universe had all kinds of names for land-based, multi-passenger transports. "Won't they question why we travel at night alone?"

She didn't so much as see as felt his shoulders slump. "Maybe we can try an autonav. It's an autonomous vehicle that you can rent, and it doesn't ask questions."

"No questions? None?" She found that hard to believe considering how strict the Pholatian Protectors were. "Won't your police watch for me to leave here?"

"Well, hmm. You might be right." He stroked his chin, then glanced at the sky. "It's about five hours until dawn. We can take my ecobike. It can go up to fifteen kilometers per hour and the Spire Wilderness is only twenty-five kilometers away. That will give us enough time to hike to a safe spot and for me to get back home before my parents wake."

Her insides fluttered. "And your ecobike? It can't be tracked?"

"Only certain public transit or government-owned vehicles have trackers. No one puts them on ecobikes."

"What if it's stolen? How do you locate it?"

J.D.'s mouth curled as though he thought her question was funny. "Theft is rare in Pholatia."

"Oh." She looked down at the ground. Pholatians didn't steal, but people like her did. He should be condemning her, not helping her. "Do you have it, or must we travel to your home?"

"It's up there." He pointed to the ledge. "I hid it with some junk behind one of those shops."

She bounded to her feet, loosening a few pebbles. "We go, then."

He rose more slowly. "You sure? If you're more comfortable hiding out here, I'll still help you."

She clenched her fists. Scoundrels had threatened them, and the night wasn't even half over. Although she feared wild animals, at least they weren't likely to attack out of malice or greed. "I'm sure."

After he stuffed the thermal blanket back into his pack, she led him to her belongings. Despite the darkness masking their movements, she kept low as she donned her extra clothes. The bulky layers would make it hard to move, but hopefully they wouldn't need to do any more running.

She grabbed her other things, leaving the fabricor and the protective thermal blanket over it. After putting all the rocks back over it, they navigated the boulders to the top. He located his ecobike and added a flat piece of junk to the seat to make it bigger. With a bit of tinkering, they both fit without too much discomfort. She wrapped her arms around his waist. Then they rode off into the night, Zahir alternating between flying or hitching a ride on her shoulder.

Other than having to veer off the streets to avoid a few nighttime drivers, they made good time. Soon, they left the city behind. The stars above dazzled even more. Not as brilliantly as they did in space, but enough to provide comfort. Maybe there really was some sort of god out there watching over her.

The air was much crisper, but the thermal blanket tied around her made it bearable. J.D.'s back warmed her other side. Being this close to him felt both good and awkward at once.

The long, straight highway lined with fields allowed them to spot oncoming vehicles and hide. When trees appeared and the road curved more, not even the night lights of those cars gave them enough notice to evade detection. Four vehicles passed them by. Fortunately, none of them slowed. And thankfully, not a single wild animal broke from those impossibly tall and spooky trees.

It seemed like forever, but J.D. eventually pulled off onto a gravel road. A few minutes later, he stopped. He set the ecobike behind some bushes and against a tree, then took her hand. She didn't see the trail until he led her into it. It was like the blackness

51

had swallowed her whole. But his self-assurance kept her feet moving.

"Sh-should we utilize my light?"

"Let's keep it off until we're farther from the road. Don't worry. I know this trail well enough."

Zahir left her shoulder. He didn't turn off his camouflage, making her wonder whether he also feared predators. Only the flapping of his wings indicated his trajectory. A pang formed in her chest as every sense of him disappeared into the night. She tried not to worry. She was his friend, not his master. Besides, he never strayed far and most likely had gone to scout the area for her.

A deep hoo noise resounded through the treetops, making her flinch. The rustling of leaves made it difficult to tell where it came from or how big its creator was. For all she knew, some giant creature lurked above and stared at her with intent black eyes. Something like the sand grylli but different added to the din. Shadows jumped as the wind blew. A rhythm like tiny footsteps echoed from the left, then halted.

J.D. pulled her hand close. "Hey. It's alright. As long as you hear the cicadas, there's not likely to be any predators about."

"Cicadas?"

"Yeah. That loud chirring... It comes from thousands of insects."

"Thousands?" She shivered.

He chuckled. "They won't hurt you. Actually, if you run out of food, they're a great source of protein. Even the larger predators like them, which is why they'll go silent if one is around."

She swallowed. The idea of eating bugs didn't bother her. It was the thought of them climbing all over her while she slept that made her skin crawl. But she didn't say anything.

"Hey," he said after several minutes. "Give me your light now."

She fished it out. He flashed it about, then pushed aside a leafy branch. "This way. Step carefully."

She kept her eyes to the ground, but not just to see what she stepped on. The shadows above had grown more menacing. The brush was thick, and she had to duck or step over several branches. Before long, they reached a rocky wall. J.D. aimed his light upward. The rock was tall, taller than the trees, and thin. *So this is why they call it Spire Wilderness.*

He led her around where two other spires crowded together, leaving a bushy gap. "It's not the best hiding place since it's close to the trail, but it will do for the night until I get you further in."

She held the light while he cleared some of the rougher brush and brought in some grass and leaves. Before long, she had a wild bed. It appeared cushier than she'd expected.

He found a hefty stick and handed it to her. "I don't have my knife yet, but this will help if any creature tries to come in here."

Her mouth went dry. She must've looked terrified because he grasped her shoulders and gave her a reassuring squeeze. "It'll be alright. The only predator big enough to worry about is a spire cat and they generally stay away from people."

"W-what if they don't?"

"They don't hunt in packs either, so if one comes this way, it'll be to investigate. Just whack it with this stick and it'll back off."

Her pulse went haywire. "How are you certain?"

"Trust me. Predators want an easy meal, not something that causes it pain. And I've been in these woods hundreds of times. The only time I had trouble with a spire cat was when I accidentally stumbled too near a den of cubs."

She didn't ask him what if it was really hungry. His face was too honest to doubt. Zahir's return gave her additional confidence. She nodded, then resigned herself to her temporary shelter.

When she'd settled, he bid her goodbye until morning, then left. She kept her light on for a little while longer before curling up under the thermal blanket. Zahir nuzzled in beside her, lending to a yearning illusion of being home. Fatigue wrapped its tendrils around her. Although numerous night sounds jittered her nerves, the chirring of the cicadas promised peace.

She finally gave in and fell into a deep sleep.

12
Back Home

The ecobike ran out of energy about two kilometers from home. J.D. pedaled down the street like a madman, his legs burning with the exertion.

A pink and purple haze rose on the horizon. All the stopping and hiding had taken more time than expected. The fear of getting caught choked him. Not that he was afraid of punishment. He could handle being grounded. It was that his parents would keep such a close eye on him he wouldn't be able to return to Fadwa.

His mom was probably awake by now, drinking her morning tea. His dad would likely be in the shower. After that, he'd sit in his home office and review his calendar. If they checked on him, they'd see the lumpy ruse he'd made in his bed. Knowing them, they'd be too angry to speak to him until evening. But if Matz came into his room to pester him and found him gone... He gritted his teeth and tried to summon a second wind. *Please still be sleeping in.*

A fiery glimmer peeked over the horizon, heralding the dawn. Fatigue pressed down on him, but he dared not slow. Only a quarter mile more.

He turned onto his street and halted. The blue lights of a Pholatian patrol car flashed from four blocks down. *Oh crap.*

He wheeled about, then took the parallel street down. The ache in his legs threatened to kill his momentum, but he forged onward. Keeping a vigilant eye out for protectors kept exhaustion at bay.

After dropping his ecobike in front of Mister Davidi's shrubs, he ducked down and crept around the edge until he came to a wooden gate. A snuffling underneath indicated Spunkster was out.

"Hey, bud," J.D. said to the dog. "It's me. Do you mind if I come in?"

The dog whined and J.D. imagined its tail wagging furiously. He'd taken care of Spunk often enough that they were good friends.

He clicked the latch and opened the gate. A metallic groan of the hinges made him grit his teeth. *Please don't let Mister Davidi be outside.*

He tiptoed through the gate. Spunkster wiggled his behind and peered up at him with eager brown eyes. J.D. knelt and rubbed the ruff around the dog's neck. Spunk turned about, showing his back end to request a good scratch above the base of the tail. J.D. complied, giving just enough attention to keep the pup from whining.

Instead of cutting across the backyard, J.D. edged along the fence and hoped Mister Davidi wouldn't be looking outside. He took it slow, not wanting to excite Spunk. When he reached the trunk of the great oak tree, he puffed and slid behind it. Peering at the back of the house through a wide window revealed no one so he hurried to the shed. Spunk followed, tail wagging.

J.D. wove around empty planters, garden tools, bricks, and other junk piled up along the side of the structure. Behind it, where old timber had been discarded, was harder to navigate. Plus the foliage had grown to as high as his waist. At least the lumber gave him a way to get a boost up over the fence.

He stepped between the area where two beams met and peeked over into the other property. His own backyard was clear of clutter. However, his mom's raised garden offered the promise of concealment.

After making sure nobody was near any of the windows, he leapt over and ducked behind the broad-leafed kale. They were just tall enough to hide him but only if he crawled on his hands and knees. The squishy ground indicated his mom had watered recently, but getting mud on his pants was the least of his worries.

He crept to where the tomato plants grew. Sweat beaded on his brow despite the crisp air. At the end of the tomatoes, he paused and listened. Other than the rustling of leaves and the chirping of birds, the morning was quiet. He darted past a gap to the trellis where vine vegetables snaked upward and halted.

No alarms sounded so he moved on. At the corner of his house, his muscles almost gave out from relief. *So far, so good.*

He edged along the wall to the back door. Peeking through the window revealed an empty dining room. *Perfect.*

He grasped the knob and prayed his mother had left it unlocked after watering her garden. His sweaty palms made it difficult to turn. He held his breath and tried again. It clicked.

Thank goodness. He huffed. With the slinkiness of a possum, he eased open the door and crept inside.

His dad's voice carried from the front room, which fortunately wasn't visible from here. "He probably went to find that ragamuffin girl." His dad's tone held that same unreasonable hate. "I want them found. Do you hear me? I want her arrested. She'll face charges right along with her family."

Arrested? The roaring in J.D.'s ears didn't allow him to catch the protector's response. Whatever guilt he felt for sneaking out vanished. He slipped into the kitchen, further from his father's poisonous attitude. The pantry was already open, making it easier for him to quietly fill a grocery bag with snack bars, freeze-dried and dried goods, and canned vegetables. Those last ones were heavy, so he only grabbed a few.

"What are you doing?"

J.D. nearly jumped out of his skin. "Shh," he hissed at his little brother who stood at the entry. "I don't want them to know I'm here."

"Why not?" Matz whispered, his brows drawn in. "Mom's been crying and dad's furious."

J.D. puffed out his cheeks. "It's complicated."

Matz crossed his arms. "Tell me or I'll tell them you're here."

J.D. clenched his teeth. He considered making his own threat, but perhaps this situation required something more delicate. He ran his hand down his face to give him a moment to think. "My friend is in trouble. She's all alone and needs my help."

"Dad says she broke a protector's nose—"

"It was an accident."

"—and stole a nano-fabricor."

J.D. fumed. "Dad's lying." When Matz's brows scrunched, he added, "He doesn't believe her family should have it."

"Why not?"

"I can't explain right now." J.D. rested his hand on his brother's shoulder. "I have to go help her."

Matz's eyes turned down. "Are you running away?"

"No." J.D. gave his brother a gentle squeeze. "I'm just bringing her some food and stuff. Please don't tell mom and dad I was here."

Matz bit his lower lip. His eyes reflected the conflict that must be warring inside.

"Please?" J.D. asked. "She needs my help. I'll be back. I promise."

His little brother didn't answer right away. But when he did, his voice held conviction. "Alright."

J.D. sagged with relief. As he hefted his pack on his shoulder, he realized he needed camping stuff too. Unfortunately, all his gear was at his friend's house. Since Micah had actually gone on the group campout, he wouldn't be home to get it for him. Not that it was a good idea to go there anyway. Not with the Pholatian Protectors out looking for him. "Can you do something else for me?"

Matz pulled back. "I don't know. I don't want to get in trouble."

"You won't. It's simple. Just go to the basement. Grab some of your camping gear. Flashlights, a thermal blanket, the canteen with the filter, your camping knife…" He tried to think of what else he could use that would be easy to carry. "Whatever you can fit in a pack."

"You're going camping?"

"No," he lied. Even though his little brother was cooperating, he didn't want him to know where Fadwa was. "I just want to get her some supplies so she can take care of herself."

Matz glanced over his shoulder and licked his lips. "How do I get it to you? They'll see me with that stuff and ask what I'm doing."

"Shove it out the basement window."

Matz dipped his head, then left. J.D.'s shoulders fell. His little brother could be a tattletale sometimes, but he could also be fiercely loyal.

Voices still carried from the front room, but his thudding heart kept him from catching any part of their conversation. He made it outside, then hovered at the steps to make sure no one came out. Then he snuck over to the single basement window and hunkered down.

It seemed to take forever, but Matz finally unlatched the window. He stood on a storage bin but still had to stretch upward. J.D. leaned in and grabbed the things. The knife in its sheath nearly dropped but he snatched it just in time.

"Thanks," J.D. said. "You don't know how much this means to me. I owe you one."

"Heck yeah, you do."

Sneaking away and getting back through Mister Davidi's yard seemed to take forever, but it also passed in a blur. He reached his ecobike without incident. Hope sprouted further when he noticed its energy level. The morning sun had provided only a ten percent charge, but it was enough to get him out of the neighborhood—and give his legs some time to rest.

I'm coming, Fadwa. Hang on.

13
Spire Wilderness

Fadwa snapped awake and bolted upright. Something was out there. She strained her ears only to be bombarded by birds and the rustling of leaves. How could anyone hope to hear anything significant out here?

Then a warbled noise drifted over. Laughter? She focused. The clipping of two distant voices carried along the breeze.

She elbowed J.D. He mumbled without waking. She remembered him collapsing beside her in the early grey morning. Now the sky was bright blue. The sun was about a quarter of the way up or down. Since she had no understanding of planetary cardinal directions, she couldn't figure out which.

Elbowing him again, harder this time, elicited a groan.

"Wake up," she hissed. "Someone comes."

His eyes fluttered open. He pushed himself into a sitting position with a stifled moan. "Where?"

She pointed. "That way. They speak of frogs."

J.D. rubbed his face with his hands and sank forward. "They're not Pholatian Protectors then."

"No. Two boys. Possibly our age."

J.D. huffed. "That explains why they're talking about frogs."

"Should we go?"

He glanced about. "Yeah. How far away are they, do you think?"

"Perhaps half the span from our meet-up place to the control tower."

"You can hear at that distance?"

She shrugged.

He shook his head. "Alright. Let's clear out. If they get closer. Let me know."

When she stood, something rustled beside her. She jerked aside. A variegated green tail appeared from under the leaves. No, not a tail. A primordial fear triggered her to gasp. "What was that?"

J.D. chuckled. "It's a snake. A mud-faced brush snake, to be exact."

"I-it slept with us?"

"Don't worry. It's harmless. It probably just needed some warmth."

"Do snakes find sleep in our beds much?"

"Naw. You don't have to worry about snakes. It's the centipedes you need to stay away from."

"What are centipedes?"

"They're like bugs."

She cocked her head.

"Multi-legged insect-like creatures," he added. "Most are harmless but the black-headed crawler can give a painful sting. Maybe even make you sick."

Her mouth dropped open.

He waved both hands as though warding her off. "Don't worry. As long as we don't sleep in moist areas, we'll be fine."

After she got her racing heart under control, they put on their packs and headed out. Zahir flew ahead, his nano-infused feathers swirling from the blue of the sky to the mottled green of the foliage to the speckled browns of the rocks.

At eye-level, the forest looked like any other. But then she glanced up and gasped. Rocky pillars reached up to the clouds like impossible columns. Their height barely exceeded the spaceport's control tower. But unlike that structure, nature had made these. And there were dozens of them.

As she and J.D. wound around one, the land dipped lower, and a hundred more sprang into view. No wonder they named it the Spire Wilderness. "Stellar," she whispered.

"Amazing, huh?" J.D. asked.

She nodded then snapped her mouth shut. "It's a city of stones."

A broad grin spread across his face. "Wait until you see Gemstone River."

Although they followed a trail that sloped downward, they did a lot of climbing too. Most often, rocky ledges created natural steps up or down. But sometimes they climbed boulders taller than her ship. To keep strong in space, her father would activate the grev-sim machine whenever their energy stores allowed. Exercising was mandatory during those times. Aymen and Taz grumbled, but she loved it. She'd jump, climb, and bound about the ship as though the floor were on fire. She'd also practice when they made landfall. But this required more exertion than she was used to, especially with the heavy pack on her back. Her breaths deepened and an ache developed in her chest. She dared not let it show in front of J.D., who traipsed along with an unwavering poise.

Before long, the breeze carried the sound of burbling water. She almost relaxed in relief, but then Zahir returned in a blur of near camouflage. "Three people ahead," he said.

Funny. She should have heard them. The noise of the forest must've overloaded her senses. After all, she wasn't used to this wild cacophony.

J.D. waved her to a narrower side trail—a trail that required more climbing. She followed without outward complaint while her mind protested. Zahir flew off again, scouting ahead.

"Why do we go up?" she asked. "Don't rivers flow down?"

"Yeah, but you'll get a good view from up high."

"All this is only for a view?"

J.D. hesitated. "Um, yeah. I thought you'd want to see it."

"But mustn't we must search for a place to sleep?"

Her anguish must've shown. His already crooked mouth twisted in what she guessed was chagrin. This place was his home. He only wanted to show it to her, and now she'd insulted him. "I'm sorry. I'm not used to this."

He ran his hand through his hair. "I'm the one who's sorry. I wasn't thinking."

"It's okay," she replied. "I want to view."

"You sure?"

"Yes. If no people are there."

He smiled. "I doubt it. And there's a place up there we can rest."

She dipped her head. He led on once more. The steep climb didn't give her much trouble until she reached a ledge barely within reach of her fingers. J.D. hauled himself up without effort. Seeing her consternation, he gave her a half-smile and lowered his hand. She grasped it and let him pull her along.

She collapsed on a small flat area of ground, panting.

"Are you alright?"

"I'm fine. Let me capture my breath."

He sat beside her, hugging his knees. She forced herself into the same position. When her breathing normalized, he pointed to the right where the Spire Wilderness spread out toward the horizon. Her jaw dropped. It was a jungle of mismatched towers. The bands of color layered through the spires reminded her of a giant orange and brown gas planet she'd seen once.

"You think that's amazing," J.D. said, "check this out."

They scooted about a meter over to the rim. She mimicked him as he rolled onto his stomach and peered down. The sight made her eyes pop.

Gemstone River lived up to its namesake. Glittering colors of garnet, lapis, emerald, and amethyst snaked through the rocks, making her gasp. "Are they real crystals?"

He chuckled. "No. It's from an underwater plant. It only grows like this once a year and for a very short time, so you're lucky you're here to see it."

Lucky indeed. She regretted being disgruntled about all the climbing. As she studied the winding rainbow, she realized he was right. The glimmer was an illusion created by the sun reflecting over the rippling water. The spectacular splendor subdued her worries. "Nothing in the entirety of the galaxy matches this."

J.D. beamed.

She beheld it for a long while, getting lost in the dazzling haze. Two adults and a child walked a path along the river below. They were likely the same ones Zahir had seen. She didn't hear them above the gurgling water. If they spoke, she probably could. But even they recognized there were no words for such a serene moment.

After a long rest, they edged away and headed back down. She found a rivulet of water containing the plants along the way and stuck her hand in. The illusion of gems shattered. The otherwise ordinary leaves were round and about the size of her pinky nail— and soft. She scooped up some water to drink, but J.D. pressed his hand down over hers, stopping her.

"Is it poisonous?" she asked.

His mouth quirked. "No. But you should never drink water from any wilderness without filtering or boiling it first."

"Why not?"

"Your body isn't adapted to the microbes."

"If you can't come here, what will I drink?"

"I have a canteen with a filter you can use."

"Oh." *Good idea.* If he hadn't been here to warn her... She shivered. What else was there out here to beware of?

"Come on," he said, holding out his hand. "Let's find a place for you to stay."

She grasped his palm, wishing she wouldn't have to let go later when he left her.

They hiked away from the river. J.D. showed her safe plants to eat and ones to avoid. All the information was helpful, but she held no hope of remembering it all. She decided it was best to rely only on what they'd brought. That would only work for so long, though. And only if he continued to come see her.

Once back amid the cluster of spires, she arched her head this way and that, looking for a place to provide cover. "What if we climb?" she asked, pointing at a spire with a base as wide as her ship.

"Not a good idea. Spire cats hang out up there to look for prey. Though I doubt they'll mess with you, they might scare you into falling. Plus, you could get stuck up there. It's easier to climb up than down."

She suppressed a groan. They kept hiking until she spotted a deep alcove. The towering spire above it seemed precarious. What if it collapsed? Or toppled over and trapped her? *Well, it's held up this long.* "What about there?" she asked.

J.D. pointed to the ground. "See that?"

She leaned over and squinted. "What?"

"That bush with the greyish leaves. It's called a grey nettle and it'll give you a painful itch if you touch it."

She scratched her hand and frowned.

"And there." J.D. waved to the opposite side of the gap. "Bones. A spire cat probably lives there. And if it's a she and she has cubs, she'll be very upset at you for going in there. I've learned that the hard way."

"Oh. Possibly we should go, then." She stumbled back and landed hard. She grasped the edge of a large boulder and pulled herself up... And came face-to-face with two beady eyes. "Aaah!"

She fell again. The arm-length creature scrambled away, its mud-green tail swishing behind it.

J.D. rushed to her side. "Did it spit on you?"

She frantically brushed her face. "I-I don't know. What was that?"

"It's a spiked-tailed spitting lizard. Their spit will burn your skin."

The air seemed to thicken. She couldn't breathe. Her head dropped into her hands. Tears spilled down her eyes.

"Hey. It's alright." J.D. wrapped his arm around her. "It's not dangerous—just hurts."

"It's not alright!" she yelled, no longer caring if anyone heard. "I can't remain here. Centipedes with poison, nettles that sting, spire cats who anger, and now a lizard that spits! How is this better than your juvenile detention center? Return me to the shipyard!"

Zahir flew back in with an angry squawk. He perched on a rock beside her and cocked his head. "Fadwa okay?"

She couldn't answer so J.D. answered for her. "She's just overwhelmed."

That's an understatement. Despite wanting to get away from here, the weight pressing down on her kept her from rising. She pulled her knees to her chest and lowered her head. She didn't want to cry, but a pressure from deep within surged outward until she was bawling.

*****

J.D. patted her upper arm, attempting to provide comfort while the pit of his stomach tumbled like grinding rocks. "I'm sorry. I'm so sorry. I didn't realize how hard it would be."

He ran his hand down his face and tried to see it from her perspective. She'd never come across wild animals unless they were caged. Spaceships didn't carry poisonous plants. The only predators were human, but at least she had her family to protect her. Here, she only had him.

For how long, though? He had intended on returning home. But if he did that, his parents would make sure he stayed there. Besides, why should he go back right now? He was already in trouble. Nothing he did would change that.

Seeing Fadwa curled in on herself and sobbing made his heart hurt. No way would he leave her like this.

Zahir hopped a step, then flew to her shoulder and nuzzled her cheek. J.D. found its soft cooing noises endearing. She was lucky to have such a good friend.

Eventually, her cries turned into sniffles. "I'm sorry," she said, peering at him with red-rimmed eyes. "I only find much scariness here."

"It's alright. I'm the one who should be sorry. I should've known it'd be too much."

She shook her head. "Yes. Too much. Not just the animals, but all. My family. Your police. Those scoundrels…" She flicked her hand upward. "This place with its strangeness."

"You know, the animals aren't that bad. They'll leave you alone if you leave them alone." He cringed at his own words, sure that he sounded condescending rather than comforting.

Other than her sniffles, silence lingered until she wiped her nose with the back of her hand. "I didn't mean it," she finally said. "I have no desire to return to the shipyard."

He sagged against her in both relief and solace. They sat quietly for a while longer as the sky turned a darker shade of blue. Only one more hour to find shelter. After that…

He swallowed down the hardness forming in his throat. He wanted to stay with her, but what about Matz? J.D. had promised to return. And what about mom? Matz had said she'd been crying. The thought twisted his insides into impossible knots. He was too angry to care how his dad felt, but it still hurt to know that things would never be the same between them again.

Fadwa was right. This was all too much. It never should have come to this. A heat ignited within his core. With his thoughts spinning, he hadn't paid attention to his surroundings. Although they had been heading downward, the land continued to dip lower. A dark line on the distant horizon caught his eye. It might be a storm passing them by, or it could head this way. He wished he had checked the weather before bringing Fadwa here. Thunderstorms tended to hit rather hard in this area.

Matz will understand. Maybe mom will too. To heck with dad. "I'll stay with you," he said.

65

She locked her attention onto him with a hopeful expression but didn't speak.

"I'll stay with you," he repeated. "Until this is over. And I know you're safe."

"W-what will your parents do to you?"

He shrugged. "They'll be angry with me for a long time, but I don't think there's anything they can do to me to make me regret helping you."

"Are you certain?" she said in a rising tone.

"Yeah." He grasped her hand and squeezed. "I'm sure."

Her cheeks turned pink. "Thank you. This means much."

Her gratitude banished all his misgivings. This was the right thing to do. He was sure of it.

14
Jellyfish Sprite

With the decision made to stay in the Spire Wilderness, a weight lifted from J.D.'s shoulders, leaving him with a heart as unfettered as a soaring bird. The way Fadwa bounded down the rocky slope suggested she felt the same. Then again, she might be anxious about finding shelter. She probably hadn't recognized the distant clouds as a storm, but darkness would fall soon.

The sun dimmed as it dipped low, sometimes disappearing behind a spire. Shaded areas of the landscape harbored a nip in the air. The wind picked up, bringing in more coolness. Its heavy, earthy scent suggested oncoming rain.

Although time was of the essence, he led her past a few potential sites before settling on one with a cavernous alcove and concealed by brush. Best of all, it held no signs of habitation.

They gathered wood for a campfire and underbrush for beds until the sky turned deep indigo. Next, he selected a spot for the firepit, where the ceiling sloped well enough for the smoke to drift outside rather than in. He knelt and constructed a ring of rocks, all while eyeing the approaching black line of clouds. Now and then, they brightened with intra-cloud lightning.

A thunderstorm shouldn't be much of a problem, but he worried about Fadwa's reaction. As he opened his mouth to tell her what to expect, a blob of glowing red sprouted high above the stormfront. Sparking red tendrils shot down and fractured the sky. The electrical phenomenon was huge, like a lake of blood and fire. J.D. straightened, nearly bumping his head on the rocky roof. "Woah!"

Fadwa followed his gaze, but the sky was black again. "What? What happened?"

J.D. expanded his lungs, trying to quell the pounding in his chest. His camping group would cut the trip short. The disturbance itself was too far up to cause harm, but its appearance denoted this storm would be dangerous. "I saw a jellyfish sprite."

"A what?"

"A jellyfish sprite appeared in the sky."

Fadwa's eyes roved wildly. "You have fish in your sky?" she asked with a squeak.

J.D. would have laughed at any other time. "No." He shook his head. "Not a fish. Not any kind of animal. It's an electrical disturbance that sometimes forms above a storm cloud. It's a sign that we're not just going to have rain tonight. There'll be lightning, high winds, possibly hail. Maybe even some flooding."

While Fadwa covered her mouth in abject terror, he took in his surroundings. They were about halfway between a high point and a deep ravine. "Give me your flashlight."

She handed it to him with trembling hands. His own panic kept him from comforting her. Instead, he went outside and studied the ground. Taking the time to investigate every area didn't take long, but it sure felt like it.

He turned off the flight and ran his hand down his face. "There's no sign of previous flooding," he said, trying to sound reassuring. *But that only means it's been a while since the last sizeable tempest.*

"Get as far back into the cave as you can," he continued. "Start piling our kindling in the pit while I find more brush."

"No!" Her head shook harder than a wet dog's. "I don't want to remain solus."

"I won't be long. I promise. We just need more cover from the storm."

"Zahir!" she called out for the scouting bird. Only crazy—or desperate—people would be out here with a coming storm.

She hugged her arms close and shivered as her eyes remained fixed on the sky. The jellyfish sprite appeared again, larger this time. She belted a scream and ducked further into the alcove.

"It'll be alright!" J.D. called out louder than intended. "The storm is still at least twenty minutes out." *Not enough time to hike out of here in the dark, darn it.*

The blur of Zahir zipped past. "Storm. Storm."

J.D. expelled a breath, grateful for the comfort the two provided one another. Using his camping knife, he hacked off a few stout branches of some nearby shrubs. The sticks by themselves wouldn't do much good but the attached foliage might. It took longer than expected—or the storm arrived sooner than anticipated. Thunder rolled and droplets of rain fell as he stacked the weaved bundles against the opening.

If he had time, he'd make them sturdier. Of course, if he'd had time, he would've found a better shelter. The alcove seemed deep enough to avoid the worst—unless this turned into a squall and blew in.

The wind picked up, pelting him with icy specks of water. Then the droplets grew bigger. Though slushy right now, it was a sign of coming hail. He gave up on securing the brush and darted inside. Fadwa had stacked some kindling in the firepit, but not quite in the way he'd intended. He reorganized it, forcing a steady pace to keep his panic from manifesting in front of her.

A gust of wind swept half his makeshift door away, but he didn't attempt to fix it. A flash of lightning illuminated the sky to near daylight. Thunder belched, making Fadwa yelp and Zahir squawk. The time between the sight and sound indicated the worst of the storm was still a few kilometers out.

He lit the fire, then blew it into a steady flame. Within minutes, it had grown enough to provide moderate warmth. Zahir kept its distance, choosing to investigate the rest of the alcove and scratch the dirt in search of bugs.

J.D. scooted closer to Fadwa and noted how haunted her eyes were as she stared at the flames. With the stretch between lightning and thunder narrowing, things were about to get worse.

She didn't acknowledge him when he nudged her shoulder. He bit his lip, trying to decide how to put her at ease while his own fears threatened to spill out. Assurances weren't enough. Perhaps a distraction. "So what's it like out there, living in space?"

"Most times, it has dullness," she replied half-heartedly.

"But sometimes not, right? I bet you've seen a lot of interesting things."

"Yes. I like viewing new places. But it has dangers too."

She didn't elaborate, so he prodded her for more. "The places you visit, or space?"

"Both." She inhaled loudly. "You know why we badly need this fabricor?"

"So it's easier to make food," he replied.

69

"It's more." Her eyes took on a distant look. "One time, we located a signal of distress. We followed it to a ship like ours. It was dead. Its engine broken. For a quarter-year, it traveled only by propulsion. Food and water ran out. Only one crewman survived. We gave him nutrition, but it didn't aid him. He died." She paused and met his eyes. "More people need this. If we all had a fabricor, our aid would not have come too late."

J.D. hung his head. He'd heard many stories much like this one, which was why most people in Pholatia, including the government, considered space travel too dangerous. *It's not worth the risk-reward ratio*, his dad had once said.

That might be true for Pholatians, but not everyone had a homeworld full of such rich resources. People like Fadwa's family survived at the whim of a harsh and vast environment. While a nano-fabricor still needed input to create food, simpler molecules that were cheaper and more condensed might've kept that crew alive long enough to get rescued.

Instead of being scared, she seemed sad. He grasped her hand. "I'm sorry. There shouldn't be anything wrong with you, or anyone else, having a food fabricor. My dad's just being a jerk." Thunder boomed as though emphasizing his point.

She flinched, but her expression held more dejection than fear. "I hope your parents don't give much punishment."

"Even if they do, it's worth it."

A series of lightning flashes followed by rumbles of ground-shaking thunder redirected her gaze to the outside. The tightness between her eyebrows returned and so did his trepidation. Storms had been known to topple spires.

It did no good worrying, so he nudged her. "Question. Why didn't the Prontaean Cooperative help those people?"

Her throat bobbed but she pulled her eyes back to his. "They would've if they'd learned of it. Even with frequented routes, space has much vastness."

That makes sense. "Maybe I'll join the Cooperative someday."

The crease in her brows softened. "Yes?"

"I could travel more. Pholatia has a lot of amazing sights, but I want to see more. Like the Verdanta waterfalls or the great Creesian volcano."

She laughed. "You can't view those from space, silly."

70

He smiled. "Naw. I know. But they visit other worlds, so I won't be in space *every moment*. Have you ever met anyone from the Cooperative?"

"Sure. Many times."

"What do you think of them?"

She shrugged. "They can have sternness but since we aren't lawbreakers, they don't give harassment."

"If I join the Cooperative, I won't be stern. I'll be fair."

"Possibly you can be a council member."

J.D. shook his head. "That sounds too much like a politician. If there's one thing I don't want to be when I grow up, it's my dad."

He paused, unsure if he believed it. If someone had asked him a month ago, he would've said he wanted to follow in his dad's footsteps. Did his words to Fadwa come out because of his anger toward his dad, or did he really mean them? In truth, he never understood why his dad belittled all the Cosmopolitans' beliefs. Wouldn't it make more sense to compromise?

"Your father doesn't have much kindness," she mumbled, looking away.

Although he agreed with her perspective, the words stung. "He's usually a great dad. I honestly don't understand why he's acting this way."

A blinding flash erupted through the night, followed by a boom that loosed rocks from the cave ceiling. Fadwa screamed and vaulted backward. Zahir leapt upward, wings flapping, and hit the ceiling with an angry shriek. J.D. flinched, nearly falling and bumping his head too. The hairs on his arms rose from the electrical charge. An odor akin to inorganic burning cut through his nostrils.

Ozone. Lightning had struck, and close by too. He edged toward the exit and peeked out. "Oh no."

"What?" Fadwa screeched. "What is it? Do they shoot at us?"

J.D. clambered back. "No. That was lightning. It struck a tree and now it's burning." He ran his hand down his face, trying to decide what to do. "We can't stay here. We have to go."

Fadwa wagged her head. "No! We can't go outside."

"The fire could trap us. And if it creates enough smoke, we'll suffocate." His mind scrambled for a solution as orange flames flickered from outside.

"We can't vacate." Terror fueled the insistence in her voice.

Maybe she was right. Thunder still raged with the fierceness of an angry god. Lightning flicked in the sky like a snake's tongue. Rain pelted the ground hard enough to scatter pebbles. Going out in that storm would be suicide.

Wait. The rain. He examined the outside fire once more. Licks of flames extended like fingers through the bars of a cage, only to get smacked down by the fury of the storm. No way could a fire take hold in this madness. Of course, staying here required its own kind of lunacy, but they had little choice.

He crawled in beside Fadwa again and wrapped the blanket around them. "We'll stay here, then. Don't worry. It'll be alright."

I hope so, anyway.

15
Political Rivals

The house comm rang like the annoying chitter of a red-bellied mockingbird. Shaul Hapker bounded to his feet. Dina beat him to the unit and pressed the answer icon.

"Hello?" they said simultaneously, her tone anxious and his laced with both worry and umbrage.

Gayleen appeared on the screen. Her eyes drooped and a heaviness lay under them. "Morning, Legislator Hapker and Missus Hapker. I'm afraid I don't have good news for you."

Dina clapped her hands to her mouth. "Have you found my boy?" she whined.

"Not yet. We're still looking."

Dina moved her palms to her chest while Shaul remained tense. "Nothing?" he asked. "You haven't found anything to tell us where he might be?" *If that girl got my son mixed up with more foreigners, I'll…* He didn't know what he'd do. Images of J.D. being kidnapped or hurt by those dregs ignited an innate fury so immense, he considered demanding lethal force against any and all perpetrators.

"But," Gayleen continued, "we may have a clue to where he went."

Shaul clenched his fists as he imagined his son being taken away in a spaceship.

"Someone reported finding an ecobike at the southern entrance to Spire Wilderness."

Dina gasped. Shaul frowned. They'd already learned his bike was missing. But why would he go there? Micah's parents had said J.D.'s camping gear was still at their house. Certainly he wouldn't go into the wilderness with no supplies. "You think it belongs to my son?"

73

Gayleen put up an image of the ecobike. It was red, just like J.D.'s. The design was the same. It even had identical, blue-striped grips.

Dina leaned in. "I think those are his decals. Can you zoom in?"

Gayleen did better than that. She replaced the image with a closeup.

Shaul scrutinized it but couldn't remember if J.D.'s bike had this sticker. "Matz!" he called. "Come here, please."

His youngest son jogged up. "Has J.D. returned yet?"

"No." Shaul pointed at the screen. "Does this decal look like the one he has on his ecobike?"

Matz glanced at it. "Yeah. That's his."

Dina stifled a cry.

Shaul moaned. "I can't believe he took her all the way out to the Spire Wilderness."

"What's wrong?" Matz asked. "He camps out there all the time."

"You heard the storm last night," Shaul said, barely having the patience to explain. "They're almost always worse in the Spires. The news even reported a jellyfish sprite."

Dina's eyes watered. "He doesn't have any camping gear."

"Yeah he does," Matz replied.

Shaul glared down at the boy. "How do you know?"

Matz's mouth dropped open and he froze. "Uh. Because some stuff is missing."

"Stuff?" Shaul planted his hands on his hips. "What stuff?"

Matz shifted his feet. "Um, a thermal blanket. My…"

"Your what?"

"Some of my camping stuff. And food, too," Matz mumbled. More forcefully, he added, "He told me he'd come back."

"Well, he lied to you and me both," Shaul replied in an accusatory tone. He redirected his attention to Gayleen. "Search the spires. I want every drone we have out there searching for him and that infernal girl."

"On it," the woman said. "We'll request that a couple of squads accompany the rangers as well."

Shaul dipped his head, not trusting himself to speak without snapping at Gayleen. The thought of this stupid lowlife girl corrupting his otherwise well-mannered son made his skull throb. *Darn it, J.D. What are you thinking?*

He suspected the answer. J.D. was likely on the cusp of two challenging developmental stages. One was an interest in girls and the other tended to inspire resistance to parental guidance. *This is terrible timing.* How in the heck children lived to become adults amazed him.

Dina burst into tears after the call ended. "I hope he's alright."

He darned well better be. Shaul was too upset to feel her worry. Of course he hoped J.D. hadn't been hurt or killed too, but this situation never should've happened. And Matz…

He scowled at his youngest son, who studied the floor as though it were a complex math problem. "I want the truth, and I want it now, young man."

"Um. J.D. came by yesterday while you were talking with the protector."

"What?" Dina shrieked. "He was here, and you didn't tell us?"

Matz's lip stuck out in a pout. "He told me his friend needed help."

Shaul flung his arms up. "That girl broke the law. Then she attacked a protector!"

Dina added to the lecture. "J.D. was out in a terrible storm last night. What if he's been killed because of this?"

"She's right!" Shaul shouted. "You should have told us."

The house comm rang once more, interrupting his rant. He answered it without looking at the id. Legislator Gozal popped on the screen.

Shaul suppressed a curse as a man with stark white hair appeared. "Legislator Gozal. What is so important that you call me at home?"

"Forgive me, Legislator Hapker," the white bearded man said with a fake smile. "You didn't come to work today."

"Because my son is missing!"

"I'm sorry to hear that. His disappearance doesn't have anything to do with helping that poor girl's family, does it?"

"Poor girl, my ass," Shaul uncharacteristically cursed. "She's a thief!"

"She took a food fabricor, which her family claims to have purchased legally."

"Even if they did—which I highly doubt—we should not allow those devices to leave this planet, and you know it."

"If they followed our rules for attaining it, it's not currently against the law for them to have it."

Shaul wanted to scream at the man. Darned Cosmopolitans and their so-called progressive views. It made no sense to put the rest of the galaxy on equal terms with their own. Protecting these dregs put the Pholatian culture at risk and this man couldn't care less.

"That may be so," he replied with force. "But they broke another law as well, so they're staying in custody for a while." *Until the law passes that keeps them from taking the fabricor.*

In that moment, he wondered what had happened to that device. Surely the girl wasn't hauling it around the wilderness.

"The infraction was minor," Gozal said. "Punishable only by a fine. Holding them like his is unconscionable, especially since you left a little girl without her family. They must be released."

"That isn't up to you," Shaul replied smugly.

"It's not up to you either." Gozal's tone carried an edge.

We'll see about that. One thing that Gozal and his ilk didn't have was broad support from the Pholatian Protectors. They knew what these outsiders were like. They saw it firsthand *every single day.* But it did no good to argue with this hard-headed fool.

"Goodbye, Legislator Gozal. I've got a son to find." *Jerk.* "And don't call my home again."

He cut the communication off. So much red rage flushed through his veins that he wasn't sure who to be angry at. That girl for luring his otherwise good son into trouble. J.D. for falling for an outsider and possibly getting himself arrested—or worse, killed. Matz for keeping secrets. Or the scheming Gozal for using his missing son as an excuse to spew his garbage.

Dina grasped his arm. "Do you think they'll find J.D.?"

Shaul filled his chest. "Yes, one way or the other." *And that infernal girl and her fabricor too.* Gozal wouldn't win this.

16

Drones & Harriers

A welcoming blue sky spanned above, bringing a warm breeze with it. J.D. stood with Fadwa at the base of the splintered tree. Zahir hopped down from the upper limbs and peered at the charred maw where the trunk had split in two. The fire had spread to a few lower branches before the storm had doused it, but the tree might yet survive.

"We were lucky," he said as he noted all the brush lying between here and their hideout.

She didn't reply. She stood as wooden as the tree with her eyes glazed over. He grasped her hand and hefted one of their packs onto his shoulder. "Come on. Let's go fishing."

Her eyes came back to life and her brows scrunched. "Why must we fish? We have food."

"For just in case. Besides, it'll be fun."

"What if someone views us?"

"We have your hearing and Zahir's sight. If anyone comes too close, we'll have time to get away."

Neither doubt nor excitement replaced her low spirit as she let him lead the way. J.D. tried to counter her mood by pointing out the singing birds, the cloudless sky, and the bright purple flowers that had bloomed after the storm.

Zahir seemed to enjoy the tour as he investigated, but nothing worked on her. Not even the view of the Gemstone River, which had become more vibrant after swelling with rain. At least she paid attention as he made a fishing pole and set the hook while Zahir got bored and flew off.

They settled on a ledge, their feet dangling just above the eddy. Its deepness promised fish, so he dropped the line. After showing her what to do if she felt something tug at the other end, he handed her the make-shift rod and waited.

Dawn Ross

Neither of them spoke as the sun drifted across the sky and the breeze carried the fresh scent of earth and foliage. He leaned back with his hands behind his head and watched the wisps of clouds drift by and the occasional birds glide overhead. A hawk sounded somewhere in the distance, eliciting a sense of wonderment and freedom.

Zahir returned and tucked himself between them. Even though the bird had camouflage, it's instincts to hide from predators prevailed.

"I captured one!" Fadwa said.

J.D. bolted upright. "Alright. Keep a hold of it, like I said. Let him fight it for a..."

Fadwa lost her grip. The pole plunged into the water. J.D. jumped after it. The coldness enveloped him, making him feel alive. He groped for the stick and got lucky as the line caught on his leg. He grasped it and rose back to the surface. Fadwa perched over the edge with wide eyes. "It's alright," he said. "I got it."

"You can swim?" she asked, her voice full of awe.

"Of course."

"You gave me fright." She burst into laughter, a pleasant departure from her earlier mood.

He boosted himself onto the ledge and shook, spraying water everywhere and making her scream with more laughter. After hauling up the fish, he held it up with a grin. "I saved it."

She giggled. "You have much cuteness when you smile."

Despite the chill of the breeze against his wetness, his cheeks burned. This day couldn't get any better.

Her attention snapped to the left and her mirth cut short. "Someone comes!"

He unhooked the fish and dropped it back into the water while she grabbed their things. They raced toward their hideout, her bounding up over boulders with the fleetness of a spire cat and him barely keeping up despite his hiking experience.

"How close are they?" he asked, his breaths heaving.

"Not close." She glanced up at a nearby spire. "Zahir! Go search."

The blur of the bird took off in the direction she pointed. Then she halted and cocked her head. "What's that?"

"What?" He came up beside her and listened.

78

"It…" Her eyebrows furrowed. "It sounds like a whine… Like a machine."

"Oh crap. Drones."

Her eyes popped. "Yes! That must be it."

He grabbed her hand. "We have to get back to the cave. Those things have infrared."

They jetted off once more, J.D. leading since he'd already memorized the terrain. Hyper-focus kicked in and he practically flew through nature's rugged obstacle course. Although the land sloped upward, they hopped down almost as often as they climbed.

"They come—" Fadwa panted. "—closer."

"Close enough to see us?" he asked as he glanced at the sky.

"I have no certainty."

"Are they headed this way?" He legged up over a boulder. "Or does it seem like they're still searching?"

She bounded over the same rock but didn't answer. He could only guess that she was trying to find out. One moment her face pinched in concentration, the next her expression lit up. "Zahir attacked it!"

At first, J.D. whispered a silent curse of worry. Then he remembered how hawks attacked drones all the time. Whether Zahir was camouflaged didn't matter. Search drones didn't have cameras on top and so the viewer would assume an aerial assault.

He and Fadwa made it to camp. He took down what remained of the protective foliage across the entrance, knowing it would give them away. Making sure they'd left no other signs of their presence came next. Although there were a few muddy patches nearby, even in their haste they'd been careful to only step on rocks.

"Come fast!" Fadwa called from inside. "Another drone!"

He darted in beside her and held his breath. Moments passed. He listened intently. The breeze softened the twittering of birds and the buzzing of bees as it caressed a million leaves. *Wait.* The buzz wasn't just insects. It grew louder, its hum growing into a high pitch. He clasped Fadwa's hand and squeezed.

The buzzing abated. "Is it leaving?" he asked anyway.

"Yes. But more can arrive?"

He hung his head. "Yeah. Probably. They know we're out here." He hoped Matz hadn't told on him. Then again, he couldn't blame his little brother. Matz was likely worried too since J.D. hadn't returned as promised.

"What do we—"

Zahir swooped in, clicking like crazy.

Fadwa tilted her head. "Dogs?"

"It's alright," J.D. said to the bird. "People bring their dogs to the spires all the time. You don't need to worry about them."

Fadwa gasped. "No! They make constant barks that carry much anger."

J.D. frowned. Why would a bunch of dogs be barking nonstop? Then he shuddered. "Oh no. Harriers."

"Harriers?"

He grabbed what few things they had still out and stuffed them into the packs. "Scent hounds." When she still looked confused, he added, "Dogs that can track people by smelling their trail."

She caught his urgency and helped. They followed Zahir out. "Lead us away," she told the bird.

"To the river, if possible," J.D. said.

Zahir flew off, making his tail visible while the rest of him stayed camouflaged. J.D. and Fadwa trailed him. The bird found purchase on an outcropping of a spire and waited until they got to the top, then took off once more.

Fadwa panted, likely from both fear and exertion. "Why use dogs to track?"

"People get lost out here all the time," he said through his panting as they now headed mostly downward. "Dogs can detect scent better than machines."

"Will they attack?" she asked, her tone peppered with distress.

"No. But…" *We can't outrun them.* "But if we get in the river, they won't be able to track us." *I hope.*

"I can't swim." Her voice quavered. Tears streamed down her eyes. "I don't want to go to jail."

"We'll figure something out," he replied, not sure whether he believed his own words.

17
Slippery Slope

The hungry eagerness of hunting dogs drew near. Fadwa's breath shot out in short bursts as they vaulted down, then up, then down again. A lizard skittered away from her path. If it was one of those spitting ones, she had no time to care. J.D. had said the dogs wouldn't attack, but why else use them? Most of the canines she'd encountered in her travels were used for fighting or protection.

All this over a food machine. Pholatia was a horrible place. Never in her life did she think she'd be a fugitive. Sure, her family had to run from pirates before, but that was in a ship where the enemy was nothing more than a blip on the screen. The baying dogs were more terrifying than the oncoming missile her dad had evaded. Their barks echoed through the canyon and pricked her ears like stabbing needles.

Added to the din were determined yells, snapping twigs, and tumbling rocks. The noise of a drone pushed through as well, followed by a caw, a crash, then silence. Zahir was helping but she hoped he wouldn't take it further by attacking the dogs. Didn't those officers carry weapons? Stunners were deadly to small creatures.

They twisted through so many spires she was sure J.D. was lost. But that was the least of their worries. The determination of her pursuers hinted at a fate worse than jail. They reached another rise. J.D. led the way, leaping up with ease. Fadwa scrambled up and slipped, scraping her knee. J.D. poked his head out above her. He held out his big hand. She grasped it and let him haul her over the top.

Her viewpoint widened. Not a spire or tree was in sight for a stretch of countless meters. A field of rubble slanted down, leading to a pebbled bank, then a river at least twice as wide as the gemstone one. Her eyes took it all in, but her brain wanted to spit it all back out.

J.D. headed down and waved for her to follow.

"They'll view us," she cried.

"Not if we hurry."

The space between them widened so she sucked in a breath and dashed down the scree after him. She'd trusted him this far.

She couldn't tear her eyes from the river. The water seemed swift, but also smooth. There were no boulders sticking out or choppy waves denoting underwater rocks. Did that mean it was deep?

Her chest tightened at the memory of getting knocked into a pond on the planet Quitaru. The same hysteria that'd hijacked her brain as the water engulfed her threatened to do the same now. She didn't want to go in there, but she didn't have the power to voice it.

Her foot slipped. She spun her arms, much like the way Zahir flapped his wings when he got distressed, but it was too late. Her backside met a jagged rock. The momentum of her impact sent her tumbling sideways. She rolled down, sharp rocks stabbing into her like the serrated teeth of a blackbeast.

"Fadwa!" J.D.'s voice rang out.

She crashed into a boulder. She blinked with disorientation. Her entire body throbbed. With her momentum halted, she found first her arms, then her legs. She winced at the dull twang radiating from her knee but forced herself to move. Putting weight on it sent an even sharper pain running up her leg. She collapsed.

J.D. caught her before she dropped back onto the rubble. He wrapped his arm around her and lifted her into a standing position. Only she couldn't stand on her own. A tear in her leggings exposed a red knee. She didn't see any blood but her leg refused to hold her weight.

"Can you walk?" J.D. asked.

"No," Fadwa replied as she choked on the hopelessness crawling up her throat. "My leg."

J.D. shoulder-carried her. She wrapped her arm around his neck, trying to aid his support, and hopped. The rubble made it awkward, and she lost her footing again. J.D. lifted her more so she didn't land as hard on one foot.

Once they reached the pebbled shore, movement was easier though still clumsy. She used her injured leg whenever possible, keeping the complaints of the spiking pain to herself. Not that J.D. would notice with the hell being raised by the inbound dogs.

He towed her into the water. Despite the terror wrapping its tendrils around her, she let him. The way his arm supported her ebbed some of her fear—that is until her feet no longer found purchase.

Her throat closed as the current swept them away. Even if she wanted to scream, she couldn't.

For the second time in her life, she prayed.

Dawn Ross

18
Hoverfly

The afternoon sun sent rays of heat searing down between the
spires. Birds chirped, warbled, and screeched, creating a cacophony
of madness. Insects swarmed in droves. One flew into Shaul
Hapker's mouth as he pounded down the rocky slope like an enraged
elephant. He panted noisily and sweat beaded his brow, but not from
exertion. An inferno fueled his temper.

One would think with his son finally in his sights, he'd be
relieved. But no. That boy had the audacity to keep running with that
infernal girl.

Trapped on an open bank with harriers on one side and a wide
river on the other, they had nowhere left to run. Shaul almost
cheered as the dogs bounded toward them, yapping like gleeful
puppies. They wouldn't attack, but they'd found their quarry and
weren't about to let them go.

Then his son did something totally unexpected—and stupid. He
led that girl into the river. The pitch of the dogs' barks switched back
to urgency as they flounced along the bank.

"J.D.!" Shaul yelled while still only partway down the scree.
"You stop right now!"

If his son heard him, he didn't show it. Shaul reached the bottom
of the slope just as the swift current whisked J.D. and the girl down
the river. The dogs pursued, baying as though begging them to come
back. The handler whistled for them to return.

Shaul stormed up to him. "What the heck are you doing?"

The grey bearded man didn't even flinch. "Dogs can't keep up.
And they can't track through water."

Shaul stepped wide and planted his hands on his hips. "I want
my son caught."

84

"We'll have to regroup," the man replied apologetically but without deference. Shaul had insisted on joining this search, but he wasn't technically in charge. "Take them downstream—"

"Then take them downstream! The longer we wait, the further my son will get. Let the dogs keep chasing them."

"That's not how it works, Legislator."

Shaul huffed. "Some hunting dogs."

"Begging your pardon, Sir. But I know my job. We'll find your boy's trail again."

"Well, get to it then!" Shaul swept his arm out and cursed under his breath. "And send out another drone!" he yelled to the protectors.

"We don't have any more, Sir," a middle-aged woman with a permanently hard expression said. "The birds are extra fierce today."

"That's just *perfect*," Shaul grumbled and kicked a stone. "Where the hell is air support?"

"Two hoverflies are on the way, Legislator," a ranger with brown hair replied. He was about Shaul's age and the only one showing determination to do his job.

Shaul flicked his hand downriver. "There's a clearing down there. Have one land and pick me up."

"Sir," the lead Pholatian Protector said. A cherry-red lump sat on the bridge of the man's fat nose, signifying him as the one who had let the girl get away to begin with. "That's not standard proc—"

"I don't give a damn, Sergeant. My son is out there with a criminal and I'm going to find him *today*."

"Yes, Sir," the man replied with a tight expression. At least he didn't have the audacity to argue.

Shaul and the others marched downriver, sometimes having to fight the brush. It took only fifteen minutes, but that was a long time when taking the speed of the river into account. His son might've reached the waterfall by now. Surely he'd be smart enough to get out beforehand, but his intelligence was currently dubious.

More time would be wasted in picking up his scent again. Unless they got lucky and one of the hoverflies saw them get out, they might be here for a whole other day. *Damn it, J.D.*

He heard the reverberating thump of the hoverfly before he saw it. Breaking through the last of the brush revealed a broad stretch of

Dawn Ross

rugged land dotted with stunted shrubs. The dark green craft waited in the center. It looked like the thorax of a giant insect. The resemblance to anything in nature stopped there. Instead of wings, it had a fan-like mechanism on top. The horizontally spinning blades slowed down but still created blasts of wind.

Shaul cupped his hands over his brows to protect his eyes from flying sand and pebbles. He lowered his head and trudged against the buffeting wind. Not until he got inside did his hair settle. As soon as he buckled in, the hoverfly lifted into the air as though by invisible strings. Shaul arched his neck out of the open hatch and watched the ground shrink beneath him.

From what he understood, the dog handler would travel downriver by vehicle. Between him and the hoverflies, they'd find those runaways. And there'd be hell to pay.

19
Waterfall

The brisk water propelled J.D. down the river like a hapless leaf caught in a hurricane. If not for the waterproof packs he and Fadwa wore on their backs, the relentless currents might've thrust them beneath the surface a dozen times already.

When he'd decided on taking a water route to escape, it was so the dogs couldn't track their scent. He'd forgotten how heavy rain swelled a river into a raging beast.

His dad was probably a raging beast now too. J.D. had glimpsed him before disappearing around the bend. He'd swallowed down a pang of guilt. Now he swallowed down much more as the river swept him onward.

Fadwa coughed. Her wide eyes and frantic arm movements signified her panic. A touch of the same emotion sprouted in him too. Before long, they'd come to a waterfall—one that was too high to safely go over. If they survived the fall, they'd still have to fight the torrent above as it pounded them into the depths.

They had to get out—and soon.

He paddled and kicked with the desperation of a drowning rat, clinging to Fadwa as fiercely as she clung to him. A splash of icy water hit him full force just as he tried to gulp in a breath. Hysterics clawed at him as he retched the water back out and struggled for air. His throat caught, making it difficult. Fadwa must've had the same problem because her voice cracked between her frantic coughing.

I'm so sorry, Fadwa. All he'd wanted to do was help her. Now he was about to get her killed. *Stupid. Stupid. Stupid.* He should've thought this through. Dad still wasn't right, but J.D. could've made better choices.

As he choked, the world spun. Something touched his foot. Confusion poked through his panic. The world spun, not because he lacked oxygen. They were caught in an eddy.

He finally took in a lungful of sweet, blessed air. As the eddy swirled him closer to shore, he paddled and kicked with the purpose of a duck racing to protect her nest from a stalking cat.

Fighting the current didn't take as much effort. His feet scraped the bottom, then found purchase. He hauled Fadwa out. She doubled over, half gasping, half crying. J.D. tried to comfort her, but her emotions didn't turn down until Zahir swooped in and landed on her shoulder. Her cries turned into whimpers as it nuzzled her cheek.

"Come on," J.D. said when his anxiety overrode his desire to give her respite. "It won't take them long to find out where we got out."

The bird took off again, probably to scout. J.D. trudged along, the weight of his wet shoes and waterlogged pants straining his movements. Her leggings were at least thin, but her kurta clung to her thighs, seeming to tangle them.

They had no choice but to climb the steep, rocky bank. The ravine only got steeper downriver, and a thick copse drowning in floodwaters blocked their way upriver.

"Something—" Fadwa said, breathless as he pulled her up over a stone ledge. "—comes."

"Darn it," he replied with a huff as he planted his hands on his knees and gasped. "How many drones do they have?"

"It doesn't seem like a drone." She knelt and hunched over with her eyes closed. He couldn't tell if she was catching her breath or listening. Likely both.

"It's... it's like drums." She shook her head. "Like someone with much urgency who pounds on a door. And it comes with fastness."

J.D. scrunched his forehead as he tried to imagine her description. "Oh no." he straightened and boosted her to her feet. "It's a hoverfly."

The way her brows curled told him she didn't know what that was, but worry tilted her eyes nonetheless.

"It's like an atmospheric ship but..." He wasn't sure how to describe it. "But more agile."

Zahir reappeared, landing on a short outcropping. "Big bird. Strange bird." His synthetic voice seemed panicked. Or maybe it was the way he clumsily flapped his wings, perhaps trying to imitate the horizontal rotor blades.

Despite the fatigue weighing him down, J.D. bounded up the slope with Fadwa in tow. She stumbled. He grasped her sweaty hand, almost losing his grip. She grunted but made it up.

"We need to get to the spires." He pointed to one that peeped into their view over the lip of what he hoped was the final ledge. "Just two more meters up."

That seemed to give her a second wind. She kept pace with him as he zigzagged up on a more gradual path. When they reached a plateau, he almost collapsed with relief. But a thumping that was more felt than heard propelled him onward. They jogged toward a closer, albeit shorter, spire. Height didn't matter so long as it was taller than them. Narrower helped too. If they stayed out of the hoverfly's line of sight, they wouldn't be seen with either eyes or infrared. It might be nimbler than a plane, but it couldn't weave around every spire without significant risk. Not even the best AI anti-crash features had the ability to navigate these clusters.

The throbbing of an oncoming hoverfly coincided with his pounding heart. They still hadn't made it to the spire. Fadwa's panting turned back into sobs as the ground became rugged once more. She doubled over, her legs no doubt as rubbery as his. He still couldn't see the craft but discerned its direction. He tugged her another meter, then hunkered down behind a giant boulder.

She dropped beside him and fell onto his shoulder, bawling. "They won't leave us be!"

She was right. They wouldn't. Having already found them once, it'd be easy for them to narrow down their current whereabouts. It was only a matter of time before they closed in. Bringing her out here had been a terrible idea.

"I'm sorry," he said. "This is my fault."

His apology only made her cry more. After a few sniffles, tears burned his own eyes.

Darn it, Dad. Why did you have to be such a jerk?

20

Captured

Two hoverflies had already passed. J.D. eyed the second one as it retreated into the distance. Both headed toward the waterfall, so perhaps doubling back was their best bet. Or maybe further from the river. He glanced over to the opposite bank and wished they had gotten out on that side. The Spire Wilderness didn't continue much in that direction, but at least the ground would be flatter. An ache swelled as his upper thighs burned from exertion, the pain sharpening every time they had to climb over the rough terrain.

Can't do anything about it now. He grasped Fadwa's hand and led her around the copse and upriver since going further inland would require more strenuous hiking. Besides, this direction would bring them back to the Gemstone River. From there, they could return to their cave. Surely their pursuers wouldn't think to search that area again. It would serve them right if they continued a pointless pursuit downstream.

J.D. imagined his dad worrying he'd gone over the falls. *I hope you're regretting starting this mess.* He harrumphed. *Like that'll ever happen.*

"What?" Fadwa asked, her red-rimmed eyes full of gloom.

"Nothing," he replied, too tired and too embarrassed to relay his fruitless wish.

"One returns," Fadwa said, her voice forlorn.

J.D. groaned inwardly. So much for hoping their pursuers would focus around the waterfall. He and Fadwa had evaded detection so far, but they couldn't keep up this pace. The day was more than half over, but hours still remained until nightfall. Their wet clothes weighed them down and the occasional gusts of wind made them feel like they wore sheets of ice.

The reverberating of rotors reached his ears. They grunted and panted into a narrow slot between two boulders. She slipped in easily while he had to squeeze in. *This isn't good.* The tightness didn't allow him to duck. His upper body stuck out like the scout of a prairie dog. The semi-dark colored rock absorbed some heat of the sun's rays, but he doubted it'd be enough to camouflage himself against their thermal detectors. He swiveled his head, scrutinizing the immediate area for another place to hide.

It was no use. He had no time. His chest thudded painfully as the hoverfly drew closer. The wind from the machine's rotors kicked up, hitting his wet shirt and sending a radiating chill through his torso. Without stopping to wonder whether it would work, he pulled the back of his shirt over the top of his head and held it there. Hopefully the brown material would blend in, and its coldness would disguise his body heat.

The repetitive whump of the hoverfly blades amplified. Fadwa, crouched in the cranny, peered up at him. Her wide hazel eyes usually reflected a warmth, but now their frantic worry made him think of a fall leaf plastered with icy drizzle. He didn't have the confidence to tell her it would be alright. Besides, he was sure at this point that all his attempts to provide comfort came across as hollow promises.

The hoverfly flew low enough to throw gusts of air filled with tiny grits of dirt. His heart thumped at twice the pace of the rotors. Surely they didn't intend to land.

It approached at what he guessed was an appropriate search speed but didn't slow further. It glided past on his right before rising again. J.D. puffed. Fadwa's lips parted and she closed her eyes.

He didn't move until he was sure they were out of range. Fadwa slipped out like a nimble cat while he wriggled and wrenched himself out.

The brief downtime did nothing to rejuvenate their energy. His legs hurt more than ever. Fadwa braced her palms on her thighs as she moved. Up. Down. Over. Around. Every movement sent his muscles screaming. He was about to suggest another rest, but a faint yelp seemed to echo off the spires. He paused and strained his ears.

"Dogs," Fadwa said as she slumped against the wall of a spire.

J.D. deflated. He'd forgotten about the harriers. So much for his strategizing attempt.

The dogs must've located the area where he and Fadwa had exited the river because more barks resounded. He wanted to hurry but couldn't. It was as though the air had turned to sludge.

A flutter and a squawk announced Zahir's arrival. The bird appeared on a ledge before them as its camouflage fell away. "People coming. People coming."

Fadwa moaned. "How many?"

"Five. Three this way." Zahir looked to the left, then to the right. "Two that way."

"How far?" J.D. asked.

"Close. Too close."

J.D. met Fadwa's eyes, expecting panic and finding resignation. He felt it too.

"Follow me. Follow me," Zahir said as he flew off toward the river.

J.D. hesitated. Another ride in the rapids would be too dangerous. Fadwa clasped his hand and yanked for him to follow. Lacking better options, he obeyed.

They followed a somewhat smooth wildlife trail, though J.D.'s legs still threatened to give out. The barking of the dogs grew louder, echoing off the stones. He caught sight of one in the distance as it bounded over a rock. A man's yell reverberated from the opposite direction. J.D. almost didn't see him with his brown uniform. The ranger leapt from between two boulders onto a scree slope and yelled for them to halt.

Zahir, not bothering with camouflage this time, swooped past J.D. and Fadwa with a screech.

"No!" Fadwa cried. "Return, Zahir!"

J.D. urged her onward. Whatever the bird had in mind, his aid shouldn't be wasted.

Zahir cawed as he zoomed toward the ranger, then veered upward. At first, J.D. thought he'd crash into the spire. But he spread out his wings in a vertical hover and clawed the rocks. His high-pitched cries carried the fury of a brown-tailed eagle. A large spotted furry creature sprang from an alcove down to a lower ledge and yowled. Zahir harassed the spire cat as it growled and screeched and tried to get away. The animal vaulted once more and landed in front of the ranger. At about fifty kilograms, it presented a genuine threat. Its tufted ears laid back and it bared its teeth, the long sharp canines being the most menacing.

J.D. wasted no time finding out what happened next. He imagined the surprise of both the cat and ranger. The spire cat would either then attack the man or turn tail and run. Despite not being too fond of the rangers right now, he hoped for the latter.

He and Fadwa clutched each other's arms, taking turns helping the other up. They came to the corner of a large spire and clambered up around the edge, using rocks as handholds along the way. The bushes thickened, spreading out from between crags like butterflies taking wing. He pushed branches aside, some scratching, some poking, and some, like the nettles, stinging.

They rounded it and came face to face with two Pholatian Protectors. Fadwa released a sound between a whimper and a groan. J.D. turned about only to find the ranger climbing up after them. Considering the red-faced protectors as a bigger threat, he put himself between them and Fadwa. She clung to his back.

J.D. angled away from all three pursuers as they closed in. Before he could argue on her behalf, Fadwa yelped. Her grip on his shirt yanked off. He spun around to find a fourth person had grabbed her. Fadwa bellowed and kicked, but the protector clutched her in a tight bear hug.

J.D. lunged to free her, but another protector grasped him by the upper arm. He resisted, only to slip on the rubble. The man held him aloft before he cracked his tailbone, then pulled him into a similar hugging hold.

"Let her go!" J.D. struggled with the spitting anger of a spire cat. "She didn't do anything!"

He wrenched himself this way and that, cursing and making demands. Not even his dad's entrance made him stop.

"That is enough!" his dad bellowed. A purple vein pulsed on his temple.

"Not until you let her go! You have no right to take her."

"She's a criminal!"

"Only because you made her one! This is your fault. Her family never should have been arrested."

"Jairo Damark Haper!" his dad roared. "You will stop this right now or I'll have you arrested too."

93

J.D. flicked his gaze to Fadwa, who was now in handcuffs, and his rage doubled his dad's. He cursed like he'd never cursed before, using every bad name he could think of. Spittle flew from his mouth. "I will never forgive—"

A rock-cracking smack cut him off. A prickling sensation spread across his cheek. His dad had slapped him—he'd *actually* slapped him.

He bared his teeth at the man. "I hate you."

21
Interrogation

Everything seemed lit with a red haze. The trees. The rocks. Even the clouds in the damned sky. The Spire Wilderness had once been a haven for rumination and solace. Shaul Hapker doubted he'd never see it that way again.

He tramped over to the restrained little criminal and planted his fists on his hips. "You are in a world of trouble, young lady. Do you have any idea of the mess you've caused? People have been hurt!"

The girl hung her head. "I don't want to go to jail."

"Well, you're certainly going now."

She peered up at him, her eyes carrying the glossiness of someone about to cry. "But I committed no wrong."

"You broke a man's nose and cut his face!" he bellowed, pointedly not acknowledging the man behind him—the man who'd let this urchin get away. "That's assault—assault on a peace officer!"

"It was an accident." She regarded Sergeant Vargo. "I'm sorry. I had much fright."

"It's alright, miss," the sergeant replied.

Shaul whipped his head around and shot the man a glower. Sergeant Vargo's expression showed no hint of remorse, further inciting Shaul's ire. *I'm going to have a long talk with Captain Wexler about why this man remained on duty.* "You're taking this very well for someone attacked with a knife. *Sergeant.*"

"I didn't do that!" the girl cried, her voice frantic.

Shaul returned his attention to her and harrumphed. "A thief and a liar, I see."

She wagged her head. "It wasn't me. I give you my promise. It was my bird."

"Ha!" *The dishonesty of these dregs!*

"I believe her, Sir."

"Damn it, Sergeant!" Shaul faced the man once more and threw up his hands. "Just whose side are you on?"

"I saw her dart off right after she kicked me," Sergeant Vargo replied with a straight face.

"Then what in the heck do you propose cut you? And don't tell me it was a damned bird."

"I didn't see it, Sir. But I know I saw her retreating."

Shaul scoffed. "Yeah, that sounds likely."

Sergeant Vargo's lips pressed into a thin line, wisely keeping his mouth shut. A glance at two of the other officers suggested others sympathized with this girl, too. One officer, he couldn't remember her name, looked like she wanted to reach out and give her a hug. And the young man who'd seemed eager earlier now glanced at the ground and kicked up dust. *Pathetic.* All because of a weepy little girl who was undoubtedly a good actress.

He turned back to the sniveling child with a glower. "Where's the fabricor you stole?"

"I-I didn't steal it. It's ours."

"Not until we verify your dad's paperwork, it's not. Now where is it?"

She didn't reply. Instead, her face contorted as though she wanted to bawl some more.

"You'd best speak up, young lady. You're in a heap of trouble already. Don't make it worse."

Her mouth broke open into a cry that turned into a whimpering that grated on his nerves. "Oh, knock it off. You and I both know it doesn't belong to you. Now tell me where it is before I put you somewhere worse than juvenile detention."

J.D. pushed between him and the girl. "Quit being so mean!"

Shaul started, but his anger returned with a vengeance. "Back off right now, young man," he said, jabbing his finger. "You're on the verge of becoming a lawbreaker too. You're lucky *you're* not going to the juvenile detention center. Do you have any idea how much of a mess you've created?"

"*You* did this, not me." J.D. mimicked the emphatic pointing. "If you had just helped her and her family when I asked, none of this would've happened."

"You had no business hanging out with these ruffians to begin with. Not only did you sneak out to the spaceport without consent, but you also aided and abetted a criminal!"

"She's not a criminal! She's just a girl who's scared—"

"Enough!" Shaul roared. "I will not hear any more from you. You act like you know these people, but you don't. You have no idea the danger you put yourself in—put *everyone* in with this stupid stunt of yours. Now get your ass in the hoverfly, right now."

He glowered with a vehemence that usually made his children capitulate, but J.D. stood his ground with his arms crossed and feet planted.

"Damn it, J.D. I've had enough. Get to the hoverfly before I have you arrested too." His son still didn't budge, so he turned to the younger protector. "Escort him. If he doesn't cooperate, put him in cuffs and haul him there."

The young man's throat bobbed and his eyes swept back and forth between him and J.D. "Are you sure, Sir?"

"Yes, I'm sure. Now do it."

"Alright," the officer replied in a reluctant tone.

With a red face tighter than an old uniform, his son obeyed as well. Shaul followed as a deafening silence hung about the group like a suffocating shroud. His head buzzed with the fury of a hornet's nest.

What is it with everyone taking the side of this wretched girl?

22
Procedure

The thunderous tempo of the hoverfly's spinning blades coincided with the blustery whirlwind of J.D.'s emotions. Anger. Frustration. Even a little fear. He couldn't remember a single time in his life when he'd felt so strongly. The injustices made his head swim.

"Sit there," his dad said, pointing.

J.D. clenched his fists and contemplated defiance. This wasn't the ending he'd imagined—not even close. Nothing he did now would help Fadwa so he obeyed, climbing into the hoverfly and plopping into the far window seat with a sulking huff.

Sergeant Vargo helped Fadwa in and directed her to the seat across from him. She hung her head and complied. J.D.'s heart ached at her broken spirit.

"Wait!" Fadwa leaned over and peered outside with anxious eyes. "Zahir!"

She shouted a few foreign words that J.D. assumed were commands. He realized the bird wouldn't be able to keep up with a hoverfly. "We're going to the search and rescue base," he said, thinking she'd given Zahir instructions on where to meet her.

Both J.D.'s dad and the sergeant frowned at them like they'd gone crazy.

"Sit back, young lady," his dad said, then turned to J.D. "What's she going on about?"

J.D. pressed his lips together and looked away.

"Zahir!" Fadwa's voice pitched in desperation as she stood.

Sergeant Vargo put his hand on her shoulder but didn't seem to apply pressure. "Take it easy. What's Zahir?"

"My pet!" Her forehead furrowed, enhancing her stricken expression. "I can't leave him."

"That's enough," his dad said. "We're not waiting for some *imaginary* bird."

"He's not imaginary," J.D. replied. "You've already separated her from her family. You can't force her to leave her pet behind too."

"No. We're going." His dad signaled the pilot.

"Belay that!" the sergeant called out, then scowled at J.D.'s dad. "It won't hurt anything to wait for her pet."

J.D.'s worry about what would become of the bird evaporated as a blur swept in, creating a faint flutter. The sergeant flicked his hand by his ear. His dad cocked his head toward the sound, then curled his brows at Fadwa. J.D. held his breath as a distortion settled on her shoulder. Hopefully, Zahir remained invisible—and quiet. Even though his appearance would lend credence to her story, these people would probably use the bird's cybernetics as another reason to punish her.

He gave Fadwa a knowing look. "Don't worry. Zahir knows to find you at your ship." Boldness surged through him as he narrowed his eyes at his dad. "And I'll go check on him from time to time."

"Like hell you will."

"Unless you plan on tying me up in my room," J.D. grumbled, "I'll make sure her pet is alright." His emotions swelled with satisfaction at his dad's upper lip curled.

Fadwa kept her head down but met his eyes. He gave her a secret smile and she returned it with a slight curl of her own mouth.

"Here," the sergeant said to Fadwa. "Let me take those off."

J.D.'s dad jerked forward as though to rise. "Oh, no you don't. Those cuffs stay on."

"We've checked her for weapons, Sir," the man replied, almost sounding peeved. "And it's not like she can run anywhere from here."

"I don't care. Leave them on."

"Sir." This time the sergeant didn't hide his irritation. "I appreciate your input, but you are not in charge here. I will do my job as I see fit. And if you have a problem with the way I'm handling things, file another complaint."

J.D. wanted to cheer but settled for just smiling instead.

Sergeant Vargo took off her bonds. He plopped into the seat next to her and buckled in with a frown directed at J.D.'s dad. "Don't worry," he whispered to her. "I'm not pressing charges against you either."

Fadwa peered at him with furrowed brows. The sergeant's solemn expression seemed to have heartened her because she dipped her head.

J.D.'s dad glared at the man with the same perpetual ire. The sergeant jutted his chin in response. J.D. smirked as his dad turned away with a growl. Good to know that not everyone agreed with Fadwa's treatment. Maybe Sergeant Vargo wasn't so bad after all.

The pilot radioed in his ready for takeoff. J.D. chewed his lip, wishing there was something he could do or say to provide Fadwa with reassurance. The hoverfly lifted, making his gut tumble. The sensation dissipated as they rose higher. As the spires receded, the ground looked more like a field of rubble. The last time he'd had ridden in one of these, it had been an exciting adventure. The expanse of the landscape had awed him. Seeing its subtle changes had instilled a desire to explore it all, piece by piece.

He couldn't resurrect that feeling now. Except for the chatter from the cockpit radio, not a single person spoke during the flight. J.D. would've called the silence awkward, but it was more like an oppressive heat. He stared out the window the entire time but noticed nothing as his thoughts spun.

The trip seemed to both drag and end abruptly at the same time. As the hoverfly powered down, his dad exited first. He stepped outside with a scowl that J.D. returned with the same deep-rooted intensity. There'd been a time when his dad could incite fear, but not today. No amount of punishment compared to what'd been done to Fadwa.

He leapt from the cabin onto the concrete hoverpad. The nearby search and rescue base was smaller than expected. Just a one-story, brown-bricked building with a few windows. He supposed it didn't need to be that big with rescuers often deployed elsewhere.

He caught the blur of Zahir as he left Fadwa's shoulder and flew off. Sergeant Vargo didn't seem to notice as he helped Fadwa out. "Sorry about this," he said as he put the cuffs back on Fadwa's wrists.

"It's okay," she replied meekly. "Thank you."

His eyes tilted in pity as he placed his hand on her shoulder. J.D.'s dad made a face like he wanted to curse and spit, but he didn't comment.

J.D. headed toward the building until the sergeant grasped his shoulder and steered him in another direction. Everyone maintained the same closemouthed disposition as they marched across the hoverpad to where two patrol cruisers waited. A Pholatian Protector J.D. knew as Officer Danon dipped her head at his dad and signaled for him to get into her car.

His dad he waved her off. "I'll take my vehicle."

"That's fine, Sir," she replied. "But you must go to the Savyon Peace Station."

"What the hell for?"

"Lieutenant Nissany needs to speak with him."

"I will not have my son treated like a criminal."

"Don't be such a hypocrite, Dad," J.D. interjected scathingly. "I broke the law too. I shouldn't be treated any differently just because I'm a legislator's son."

The woman ignored him and replied to his dad with a professional mien, "It's simply procedure, Sir. We've spent a lot of resources on this endeavor, so everyone involved will need to report."

"Yeah, Dad," J.D. added. "You can't very well arrest people for minor offenses, then turn around and let me flout the law."

Fadwa snuck him a grateful look.

His dad's jaw twitched. "Damn it, J.D. If you end up in jail for this too, I won't bail you out."

J.D. suppressed a smirk. *Your hateful attitude looks different when you apply it to me, doesn't it?* But he didn't say it. He didn't need to. His dad knew it, even if he wouldn't admit it. He crossed his arms instead. "Fine with me. I don't want to go home anyway."

And he meant it.

23
Cosmopolitan

The landscape passed in a blur. J.D. rested his cheek on his fist and his elbow on the vehicle windowsill and pointedly ignored his dad's scolding. It didn't matter how hard he tried to argue the case, his dad insisted outsiders didn't deserve the same treatment as Pholatians. "*They're not the same as us,*" he'd said countless times.

The tightlipped expressions of Officer Danon suggested she disagreed, but she never spoke. She pretended to study the dashboard stats as the autopilot drove them into the city. J.D. caught her eye now and then but couldn't tell whether her brow wrinkled out of sympathy or reproach. If the former, she probably didn't want his dad's ire to turn onto her.

"At least twice a year," his dad droned, "some dreg gets the idea that abducting and ransoming one of our people is a great way to get rich quick. And damn it J.D., none of those scenarios ended well. We don't have the means to chase after a ship so we have no choice but to pay. But do our people get returned? Not after experiencing terrible abuse."

J.D.'s gut wrenched. If this hadn't almost happened to him, he would've assumed his dad was making up stories to scare him. As it was, his father threw every argument at him, no matter how feeble. This was the only one that resonated. Still, Fadwa and her family didn't deserve to be treated like crap just because of a few scoundrels.

He wondered how she was faring now. At least she rode with Sergeant Vargo. He imagined him telling her it would be alright and that they'd make her comfortable until this was sorted out. He wondered whether she believed him.

After driving past fields, one-story businesses on ample plots of land appeared. Varne's Mechanics spread out over a couple acres with an office and a row of vehicle garages in the front and maintenance hangars dotted along a landing strip in the rear. A recharge station with a convenience shop came next. And beside it was an eatery that also served alcohol.

Before long, they'd left the outskirts and entered the city proper. The patrol vehicle ahead stopped at an intersection. As J.D.'s car pulled up behind it, he craned his neck. The blur of Zahir wasn't noticeable from this distance, but he hoped it still clung to the bumper. Probably so. Fadwa hadn't seemed too concerned so he tried not to worry either.

The businesses grew more cluttered and the buildings taller. They'd traveled from two-story structures to twelve in a matter of minutes. The roads became more congested with both vehicles and people.

They passed a familiar café. Both his mom and dad worked in this area. They sometimes brought J.D. and Matz to this place when school was out but they still had to work. Matz practically drooled over their cinnamon buns while J.D. preferred the coffee his parents had decided he was old enough to drink. he also liked it when Ayla was working. His cheeks burned every time she smiled at him… Well, smiled at everyone, really.

The scene interrupted his pleasant thoughts. They'd reach the Protectorate Hall in a few blocks. That wasn't their destination, but he had a wild and crazy idea that he could leap out of the car and run in there to get help. Surely, someone would listen.

He pressed a button on the door and the window eased down. A chilly breeze blew in along with the stale scent of concrete. His dad might've told him to close it, but J.D.'s focus didn't let him hear. The next intersection appeared. Just two more blocks.

His heart pounded in anticipation as the congested traffic kept them at a crawl. The white brick building of the Protectorate Hall loomed closer. Its façade rose three stories and was topped with decorative crenellations. The two-story entrance put every other architectural structure in the city to shame. Its ornate entablature frame of robust blue, brilliant maroon, and sparkling gold led into a warmly lit alcove containing a set of double-doors tall enough to accommodate a giraffe.

The traffic lightened a bit and his car sped up. It'd hurt jumping out, but he didn't care. As soon as the vehicle reached the entrance, he lifted the door handle.

Nothing happened. He jerked it up again. Nothing. He rattled it. "What the heck are you doing?" his dad asked.

A gust of wind blew on J.D.'s sweaty forehead, making him shiver. He'd forgotten the safety feature that kept anyone from opening doors while the car was in motion. *Darn it!*

J.D.'s heart sank as the vehicle passed the building and sailed on through the next intersection. Just as he was about to give up, a familiar face caught his eye. He arched his head out the window and focused. It was definitely a white-haired man walking briskly away from the Protectorate Hall, but was it who he hoped?

"Legislator Gozal!" he cried out before knowing for sure.

The man turned about. His white beard flopped awkwardly.

It was him. "Legislator!" J.D. yelled again as the man's eyes locked onto his. "My father is trying to arrest a twelve-year-old girl." He pointed to the car ahead. "You've got to—"

J.D.'s father yanked him back inside. J.D. flipped his arm, deflecting his father's hold. "You've got to help her!"

"Get back in here!" J.D.'s dad bellowed. Then to the navigator, "Get this thing moving!"

"Sorry, Sir," Officer Danon replied. "Traffic."

Legislator Gozal fell from view. The image of his furrowed brow seared into J.D.'s brain. Had he also seen comprehension in the man's widening eyes? He couldn't be sure the legislator had heard him clearly. Had he known what J.D. was talking about? And if so, would he care? There'd been a flash of recognition when he saw J.D. but maybe he was just surprised to have someone in a patrol car yell at him.

A swirl of both hopeful and discouraging emotions spun in J.D.'s head as his dad berated him for his so-called stupidity. Perhaps it wasn't so stupid. Legislator Gozal was a Cosmopolitan— his dad's primary opponent. They took a different stance on the galactic perspective. Whether it meant Cosmopolitans saw outsiders in a positive light, he wasn't sure. But being his dad's rival might be enough. Surely there'd be a political advantage to gaining the trust of another legislator's son.

That hope held about as thin as a spider web, but J.D. prayed it'd be just as strong. Nothing else he'd done for Fadwa had helped.

Please let this work!

24
The Right Side of the Law

Shaul Hapker shot a scowl at Legislator Gozal. They'd passed too quickly for him to determine whether the man had heard J.D.'s plea. If so, he'd better not interfere. His politics were already ruining this society. Now they were influencing his son. *Intolerable man.*

He clenched his teeth almost hard enough to make them crack. The smug expression on J.D.'s face didn't help. Who was this boy? This wasn't his son.

"That infernal girl has corrupted you," he said.

J.D.'s nostrils flared. "You're the one who's corrupted. We're supposed to help people, not treat them like garbage."

"Damn it, J.D.! Those people aren't like us."

"You keep saying that." J.D.'s eyes flashed. "But we're all human, Dad. There's no us and them."

"There's Pholatians and then there's everyone else."

J.D. huffed. "You're just using that as an excuse to hate."

"I'm trying to protect our own! Pholatia has reached a state of global goodwill and harmony. These outsiders threaten that."

J.D. laughed without mirth. "Not everyone has reached a state of goodwill. You're a hypocrite."

Shaul clenched his fists. "You know of nothing outside of Pholatia. You're a naïve little boy who could've gotten himself killed."

"You taught me to be open-minded, and now *you're* telling me not to be?" J.D. replied in an incredulous tone.

"Open-minded, not blind and stupid. I told you not to go there. I *told* you those people were dangerous. And all this trouble that girl has gotten you into is proof."

J.D. punched his thigh and growled. "You're the reason for all this, not her!"

"That's enough! Your attitude is out of control. I don't even recognize you anymore. Where's the well-mannered young man I raised, huh?"

"My attitude came out when you showed your true colors." J.D. crossed his arms and glowered out the window.

"Damn it, J.D." Shaul huffed in exasperation. *Why are you being so stubborn about this?*

Come to think of it, Shaul had once been as dewy-eyed about the foreigners too. It wasn't until later in his career as a Pholatian Protector that he'd learned the truth. His new assignment at the spaceport in Chorma had revealed an onslaught of horrendous human behavior. Assaults, rapes, and an occasional murder. Hell, he'd never seen a dead body until Chorma. The memory of the man who'd been beaten to a bloody pulp still cropped up from time to time, especially now when he thought about how this could've happened to his son.

Maybe if I tell him about this, he'll understand. He sighed. Perhaps he'd bring it up later when they were both calm.

They arrived at the station. J.D. got out and slammed the door. Shaul gritted his teeth but didn't comment on it. Nor did he say anything when his son joined Sergeant Vargo in helping that ragamuffin girl out of his vehicle.

She really was a pathetic sight—skinnier than a reed, gaunter than a stray dog, and dirtier than a pig. Her greasy hair and shabby clothes made her look like she'd just crawled out of a dumpster. Sure, some of that may've been due to their little camping excursion in the Spire Wilderness, but he doubted she bathed much anyway. What in the heck did his son see in her?

J.D. hung back for a moment and stared at the rear of the sergeant's car. "Don't worry," he said to no one. "She'll return soon."

Shaul crossed his arms and frowned. *Who the heck is he talking to?* No doubt that crazy dreg had rubbed off on him.

They entered the circular lobby occupied only by the white-haired officer at the service window. "Wait here," the man said with a bored expression. "Captain Wexler will be out shortly."

Shaul almost argued about having to wait for a mere captain, but decided this man probably wouldn't care enough to change the situation.

The officer who'd driven him and J.D. led the girl to a bench set against the left wall. The sergeant and another officer stood on either side. Shaul wanted to take a seat on the opposite end of the room but planted himself on the one closest to the girl before his son got there.

J.D.'s jaw clenched, but he didn't speak. Nor did he bother making eye contact. He merely wore an expression that was as surly as Shaul's own.

Except for the rustling movements of the two standing officers, the stark silence of the room simmered Shaul's temper. Time ticked by. He bounced his knee, tapping at first, then rampaging into an agitated quiver. How dare they keep him waiting! He had a son to take home and a job to get back to. He had no time for this nonsense.

The moment he rose, intending to give someone a tongue-lashing, a rear door opened. But instead of the captain, Legislator Gozal jaunted in wearing his formal white robes and a triumphant smile.

Oh, hell. Shaul crossed his arms as the man approached.

"Good news, Legislator Hapker," Gozal said. "The girl's father was just released, along with his crew members."

The girl gasped at the same time J.D. cheered.

Before Shaul could argue, the man's eyes fell on the girl and her Pholatian Protector guards. "I must say, this is a rather severe abuse of power. Dogs. Hoverflies. Pholatian Protectors? All to capture a lonely girl whose only offense was running away to keep from being placed in one of those horrible detention centers?"

"She took my son," Shaul replied, his tone deep and challenging.

"She didn't take me," J.D. protested.

Shaul shot him a glower. That was true. His foolish son had gone willingly. Damn him. "She committed a theft," he said to Gozal instead.

"Surely you don't mean the fabricor," the man replied, condemnation laced through his voice. "Didn't you hear? Her father's purchase was legal. She only took what belonged to her."

"Those shouldn't be going off world, and you know it." Shaul jabbed his finger. "Do you have any idea what will happen when our enemies duplicate the technology?"

Gozal clapped his hand to his chest in mock ignorance. "They'll eat?"

"Don't play dumb. You know very well that in the wrong hands, that technology can be applied to weaponry."

Gozal jutted his chin. "Pholatians didn't develop this fabricor in a vacuum. Scientists all over the galaxy are developing nano-replicators. To harass a family and traumatize a little girl who just wants to eat is unconscionable."

Shaul opened his mouth to argue further but the captain's arrival halted him.

"All charges have been dropped," the robust man said firmly. "Release her."

Shaul wanted to protest but knew it wouldn't do any good. He and Captain Wexler agreed on a lot of policies, but when the man had come to a decision, no amount of badgering or threatening would change it. It made him an effective captain in most cases. Just not this one.

Damn it all to hell.

*****

J.D.'s mouth spread into a broad, gloating grin. He was right and his dad was wrong. But it didn't look as though his dad had accepted defeat. His stubbornness remained on his stony, beet-red face.

Oh well. Fadwa was free. That was all that mattered.

Sergeant Vargo smiled as he removed her cuffs. The weight J.D. had been carrying fell away, sloughed off like a wetsuit. Fadwa probably felt the same. Her eyes lit up and she shared a small smile with the man who'd once tried to capture her.

J.D. wanted to rush over and give her a hug, but his dad gripped his shoulder. He was tempted to shrug it off but settled for maintaining his joyous grin.

"Your family will be outside shortly," Legislator Gozal said.

Fadwa waved to J.D. "Many thanks," she said. "I won't forget you."

"I won't forget you either," he replied, still smiling.

She skipped out the door, her hair and tunic fluttering like a bird freed from its cage.

J.D. watched her with a bittersweet sensation spreading through him. *At least someone is glad to be back with their family.*

25
New Destiny

The video on the tablet faded from one scene to another. From the glorious Tsunami Falls on planet Matsue, to the Chestnut Dunes on Andandi. J.D. reclined on the couch in the family room and took in all the breathtaking sights. Matz played with his model engineering kit nearby. Mom was in the garden and Dad was in his office upstairs.

He relished this peace. Seventhday was the only time he had a chance to relax. No pressure from homework. No chores. Only resting and daydreaming. Some days, like today, he missed Fadwa. They'd had a lot of fun together. Even their misadventure had created fond memories. He imagined what it would be like to teach her to swim in Gemstone River, or to ski at Mount Gezer, or to canoe on Adosela Lake where the waters were crystal clear.

If only he could contact her. Galactic communication was expensive and mostly inaccessible to ordinary citizens. She probably wouldn't ever return here either. He wouldn't blame her or her family if they never came back. At least they had other places to visit—other worlds, other peoples. *Lucky*.

Despite the fallout with his dad, life was alright. He'd missed his class trip to the Chenier Islands, but being grounded wasn't so bad. His mom's overdone niceness could be irritating, but that just meant she empathized with others. Matz was sometimes a pest, but they still had fun together. And his dad... Well, he had his faults, but he genuinely loved his people. So long as J.D. avoided sensitive topics, they got along.

In hindsight, J.D. had to admit the entire escapade in the Spire Wilderness had been foolhardy. His parents were right about it being dangerous. If he hadn't been so pressured to get Fadwa away, and if he'd known Legislator Gozal would react so resolutely, he would've found a way to get the man's attention much sooner.

Dawn Ross

It took a while, but he and his dad had let go of their grudges. Their relationship would never be the same, though. There'd been a time when J.D. had wanted to follow in his dad's footsteps—become a Pholatian Protector, then a legislator. But now he yearned for more.

A soaring sensation rose in him every time he thought about visiting another world. He could travel like Fadwa. Maybe even see her again.

I'm definitely going to join the Prontaean Cooperative when I grow up.

Fun Facts

- A jellyfish sprite is a real phenomenon on Earth, though this story uses a little artistic license to make it more intense than it really is. Google jellyfish sprite and you'll see.
- The Gemstone River is inspired by a real place on Earth—Caño Cristales River in Colombia.
- The Spire Wilderness is inspired by a real place on Earth—Zhangjiajie National Forest Park in China.
- The spire cat is inspired by a tiger, ocelot, caracal, and cougar.
- Zahir is descended from ravens.
- Harriers are a real dog breed.
- The hoverfly is a futuristic version of a helicopter.

Dawn Ross

Did you enjoy this novella? Leave a review. Authors love reviews!

Does J.D. Hapker join the Prontaean Cooperative? And does he ever get to meet a dragon? Find out in the main series. If you haven't read them, search for Dragon Spawn Chronicles by Dawn Ross on Amazon.

Sign up for my newsletter by visiting my website, DawnRossAuthor.com, and get great deals!

By signing up you'll receive a short story prequel and get access to the first few chapters of the first four books.

Connect with Dawn Ross online:
DawnRossAuthor.com
Twitter.com/DawnRossAuthor
Facebook.com/DawnRossAuthor
Goodreads.com/author/show/441861.Dawn_Ross
Patreon.com/DawnRossAuthor

Dawn Ross

Books by Dawn Ross:

Starfire Dragons
Dragon Emperor
Dragon's Fall
Isle of Hogs (a novella)
Warrior Outcast
Orphaned Warrior
Fated Warrior
Spire Wilderness
(a novella)

Connect with Dawn Ross online:
DawnRossAuthor.com
Twitter.com/DawnRossAuthor
Facebook.com/DawnRossAuthor
Goodreads.com/author/Dawn_Ross
Patreon.com/DawnRossAuthor

Dawn Ross

About the Author

Dawn Ross currently resides in the wonderful state of Kansas where sunflowers abound. She has also lived in the beautiful Willamette Valley of Oregon and the scenic Hill Country of Texas. Dawn completed her bachelor's degree in 2017. Although the degree is in finance, most of her electives were in fine art and creative writing. Dawn is married and has a wonderful son. Her current occupation is part time at Meals on Wheels. She is also a mom, homemaker, volunteer, wildlife artist, and a sci-fi/fantasy writer. Her first novel was written in 2001 and she's published several others since. She participates in the NaNoWriMo event every year and is a part of her local writer group.